Dangerous
Consequences

JUN 17

DANGEROUS CONSEQUENCES

LISA RENEE JOHNSON

KENSINGTON PUBLISHING CORP.
www.kensingtonbooks.com

DAFINA BOOKS are published by

Kensington Publishing Corp.
119 West 40th Street
New York, NY 10018

All Kensington titles, imprints, and distributed lines are available at special quantity discounts for bulk purchases for sales promotion, premiums, fund-raising, and educational or institutional use.

Special book excerpts or customized printings can also be created to fit specific needs. For details, write or phone the office of the Kensington Sales Manager: Kensington Publishing Corp., 119 West 40th Street, New York, NY 10018. Attn. Sales Department. Phone: 1-800-221-2647.

Dafina and the Dafina logo Reg. U.S. Pat. & TM Off.

ISBN-13: 978-1-4967-0794-9
ISBN-10: 1-4967-0794-X
First Kensington Trade Paperback Printing: May 2017

eISBN-13: 978-1-4967-0796-3
eISBN-10: 1-4967-0796-6
First Kensington Electronic Edition: May 2017

10 9 8 7 6 5 4 3 2 1

Printed in the United States of America

This book is dedicated to Joyce Cozart. I'm strong because you were never weak. I know how to love because you loved me. I can fly because you taught me I was free. I miss you, Grandmother.

Acknowledgments

First and foremost, I'd first like to thank God for His grace, the gift of creativity, and my many blessings.

They say in life there are no do overs, yet here I sit with the opportunity to say thank you a second time. I independently published my first novel in 2011 and who knew I'd end up a part of the Kensington Publishing family. Mercedes Fernandez, thank you for taking a chance on me and for leaving me in the very capable hands of Esi Sogah who has given me unwavering support on this journey. I appreciate you both.

My husband, Dino, for believing in me no matter what; my heartbeats, Antone, Devon, Julian, and Jordan, for the gift of seeing myself in you; my mother, Elaine, all that I am is because of you; my dads, Robert and Elijah; my bonus moms, Aretha and Diana; my siblings, Sedric, RaSun, LaTrese, Marcus, Miriam Regina; my relatives—all of you are my biggest cheerleaders and I thank you for your unconditional love and support.

On most days I can be found kissing the sky (on an airplane), concocting a fabulous cocktail or living life on my terms surrounded by extraordinary friends that always have my back. Monique, Debbie, Deanna, and Aaron with those juicy stories, thank you for everything. I am eternally grateful for all that you do.

There is no such thing as a published author who took the journey alone. My book club, Sistahs on the Reading Edge—nineteen years and still laughing; my friend, Bernard Henderson the best bookseller I know; Deborah Burton-Johnson, Sharon Lucas, and Toni Bonita Robinson, I love you all tremendously; Ella D. Curry your love for books and authors is refreshing; Curtis Bunn, I am truly inspired by your love for the written word; Jane Anne Staw, without you this book would still be a figment of my imagination. Celeste Wright; Lynel Johnson Washington, I'm so glad you're on my team.

To all the book clubs and readers everywhere who have supported me on my writing journey, I'm sending you my sincerest gratitude. Thanks for taking a chance on a newbie! I hope you enjoy reading about the shenanigans of the *Dangerous Consequences* cast of characters as much as I enjoyed writing about them. Stay tuned there's more to come.

Finally, if I inadvertently missed any of you who supported me in this endeavor, please know it wasn't intentional. I am grateful and forever indebted to you. So please add your name in the following blank. _____, THANK YOU for supporting me. I couldn't have done this without you. I'd love to hear your comments. Come visit me online at www.lisareneejohnson.com.

Sending Sunshine,
Lisa Renee

P.S. I love you to the moon!

Chapter 1

Dr. Sydney Marie James panicked as her iPhone slipped out of her grasp and landed on the floor close to the front passenger door.

"Shit!" she yelled. She could hear the exchange operator's distant voice saying, "Hello? Hello?" But short of unlocking her seat belt and climbing across the seat to retrieve the phone, there was nothing she could do. She was en route to Children's Hospital, initially on her way to work, but now she was responding to the trauma call she'd just received for an infant who needed immediate neurosurgery. Frustrated, she yelled into the confines of her SUV.

"Hello. This is Dr. James. I've dropped my iPhone and can't pick it up because I'm driving. But I'm on my way and should arrive at the hospital in about fifteen minutes." She had no idea whether the operator could hear her, but it was worth a try.

The traffic ahead crawled along. Morning commuters on their way to work congested the I-580 inlet that would take her toward downtown Oakland, making traffic a nightmare.

"Come on." Sydney hissed and blew her horn in irritation. Fresh perspiration trickled down her spine and mingled with the aging sweat from her morning run. She was still dressed in black running tights, Saucony running shoes, and her favorite UCLA sweatshirt. She'd run her usual six-mile route at the Berkeley Marina, with the morning mist plummeting down on her skin and a cluster of squawking seagulls out scavenging for any sign of food lulling her with their singsong pitch, which helped to clear her mind. But that was forty minutes ago, when her world had seemed peaceful and serene...before she'd received the emergency call during rush-hour traffic.

She took her eyes off the road for a brief second to search the passenger seat, littered with CDs. She wanted to hear a Ledisi song, the one she'd played while making love to Donathan earlier and during their romantic getaway at the Highlands Inn in Carmel. The soulful music soothed her, which was what she needed on most days while commuting from El Cerrito to Oakland in bumper-to-bumper traffic.

A gap in the blockage opened up. Sydney pushed hard on the accelerator, hoping she wouldn't run into another obstruction farther ahead. She had no idea which of her colleagues was on duty. It was probably Julia Stevens. But if Julia started surgery on the incoming patient, she would be required to complete it, adding additional hours to her already-long shift. Frantic to reach the hospital, Sydney drove in an unforgiving manner as drivers on either side of her attempted to jump out of their slow-moving lanes and into hers.

"Not today, people!" Sydney bellowed. She accelerated in an attempt to prevent a red Nissan pickup truck carrying lawn care equipment from swerving in front of her.

The traffic came to a sudden halt. Realizing she was about to crash into a sea of stationary cars, Sydney instinctively slammed on the brake pedal with both feet and held her breath as she heard the tires screeching and smelled burning rubber. Her Range Rover came to a complete stop without a collision.

"Thank God," she exhaled, releasing her tight grip on the steering wheel.

Then the scream of another set of tires, a loud thud, and the sound of shattering glass punched Sydney in the center of her back. Dazed, she moved her damp, dark brown hair out of her eyes and noticed light blue smoke merging with the morning smog, along with the overpowering odor of overheating antifreeze billowing past her windows. She peered into her rearview mirror and saw a Hispanic man getting out of the red Nissan pickup she'd earlier prevented from cutting in front of her. She watched the man walk to the rear of his truck, reach into the truck bed, and remove a shovel, knocking it against the lawnmowers, the noise loud enough to make her jump. Then he hastily approached her, swinging the shovel at the air.

"*Pendeja estupida!* I can't believe you just made me wreck my work truck," yelled the man in a Spanish accent as thick as the fog that blanketed the San Francisco Bay.

"Get out of the car, you *pinche puta!*" He slapped Sydney's car window with the open palm of his thick, callused hand. The contact echoed loudly inside the car.

Intimidated by the force and vulgarity of the man's anger, Sydney stared at him through the speckles of spit on the glass that separated them. Bulging muscle cords in his neck and trickles of blood running down his forehead and pooling at his neatly trimmed mustache pointed downward to the shovel dangling from his left hand.

As bile rose in Sydney's throat, she attempted to calm down and think rationally. She glanced at the passing commuters, praying for someone to stop to help her. Instead, she found a string of spectators hoping the drama would unfold before they crept by completely and missed it.

"Open the fucking door!" the man blurted as he yanked on the door handle.

Her eyes glanced at the clock, then at the phone. She needed to call for help.

"Get the fuck away from my car," Sydney barked, hoping her angry words would bring the man to his senses.

"I'm not playing around, lady." The man began jerking on the door so hard her car rocked. She unfastened her seat belt, climbed across the middle console, and retrieved the phone from the floor. She was so nervous that instead of dialing 911, she dialed her husband. He answered after the first ring.

"I must have dicked you down well this—"

"Donathan!" Sydney screamed into the phone.

"Get out of the car, you *pinche puta!*" The Hispanic man continued his tirade, drifting in and out of his native tongue. Holding the shovel high above his head with both hands, he slammed it into the hood, repeating his assault over and over again.

"Get away from my damn car." The loud thud of the shovel hitting the hood registered through the phone.

"Sydney, who is that? Where are you?" Donathan demanded.

"I was just rear-ended by this man and he's—"

"I'm going to fuck you up just like you fucked up my truck. Get out, *pendeja*, before I smash your windows."

Sydney scrambled for her purse on the backseat. She reached inside and pulled out an old canister of pepper spray she'd hoped she'd never have to use.

"Where are you?" Donathan demanded again.

"I-I'm on I-80 about to merge onto 580." The hood of the truck absorbed another hit from the shovel.

Her eyes went wide as the man shouldered the shovel and paralleled his feet, like he was Barry Bonds readying his swing and his strike zone was now the front windshield of the Range Rover.

"Oh, God, nooo!"

Chapter 2

Frazzled, Sydney stood on the shoulder of the road as she spoke into her cell phone to the exchange operator. "I'll live."

Five vehicles were parked next to the guardrail, including two highway patrol cruisers. Sydney's eyes were fixed on the Hispanic man being stuffed into the backseat of the police car. He was clad in jeans, cowboy boots, and a plaid button-down shirt, his hair short, neatly trimmed above his ears. He looked like a normal guy, but where normal people radiated a sense of calm, this man was pulsating with anger.

When Donathan maneuvered his Harley onto the shoulder, Sydney ended her call with the hospital and watched as he parked and removed his helmet. His face was tense and his forehead furrowed as he got off the motorcycle and made his way to her.

"Are you okay?" Donathan asked, his eyes narrowed in confusion. He stole a glimpse at the hood, then pulled her into an embrace.

"Punk motherfucker," he mumbled under his breath. His tone was seething and harsh. She could feel his heart beating like it wanted to jump out of his chest, which matched the beat of her own. The possibility of becoming a road-rage statistic disturbed her as she listened to the two African American males, in their midtwenties, give their statements to the officers. They'd arrived just in time to subdue the Hispanic man before he broke out the windshield with the shovel.

"What happened?" Donathan questioned, his voice quivering with the fury he wanted to unleash.

"Honey, I'm fine. I just happened to be on the highway in front of a lunatic this morning."

Sydney rubbed her hand across her upper chest, where the seat belt had pressed into her during impact. As she took a peek inside her sweatshirt, Donathan's eyes followed. The couple stared at an almost two-inch-wide bruise that reminded her of a beauty pageant sash. "You need to get that checked out—"

"It's just a bruise from the seat belt," she said. "No big deal. I'm fine."

"Sydney, don't give me that I'm-fine crap. You might have fractured your collarbone."

She raised both hands in self-defense. "Calm down, sweetie. I'll let one of my colleagues check me out when I get to the hospital."

"Excuse me, Dr. James," one of the officers said, interrupting their battle of wills. "Here's my card. I've written the incident report number on the back. It will be a few days before the report is ready, but if you provide this number to your insurance agency, they'll be able to obtain all the information they need. The district attorney will contact you soon to discuss the possibility of filing charges. All I need is your signature on this preliminary report and you're free to go."

"File charges?"

"Yes, ma'am. In cases like this, that's procedure."

"Well, what if I don't want to file charges?"

"Of course she wants to file charges," Donathan interrupted, his face twisted with confusion. He stretched his hand toward the highway patrolman. "Thanks, Officer."

"No problem, sir. Glad we were all able to walk away without any casualties. Now, if you can just sign right here, Dr. James, you can be on your way."

Sydney nodded with understanding, took the clipboard from the officer, and scribbled her name.

Donathan made his way over to the two Good Samaritans and thanked them. Sydney stood still for a moment. *Had her erratic and aggressive driving been the cause of the accident?* As she headed toward her SUV, a wave of panic washed over her and her hands shook as she buckled herself in. What would have happened to her had the Hispanic man actually gotten her out of the vehicle? Would he have hit her with the shovel? She could be dead. Her momentary thought of being responsible for the accident dissolved. She might have driven a bit erratically to prevent the man from cutting in front of her, but by no means was she the reason he'd rear-ended her.

Donathan approached the driver's side window. "Are you sure it's drivable? We should have the highway patrol officer call a tow truck—"

"Babe, I really don't have time for that. I need to get to the hospital. The dents on the hood are from his shovel, not the impact, so it should drive okay." One turn of the key and the engine hummed to life. "See, it sounds great."

After a moment of hesitation, Donathan conceded, and then leaned through the window to kiss her. "I'll see you this evening."

Sydney took a deep breath and watched in the rearview mirror as her husband walked away.

After a few false starts, Sydney pulled away from the shoulder into the oncoming traffic. She carefully negotiated the lane switches until she was in the farthest left lane and refocused her attention on getting to the hospital. She turned up the volume on the sound system and sang out loud, trying to forget the horror of what had just happened to her.

A bright red Emergency Medical Service helicopter was lifting off the landing pad as Sydney entered the doctors' parking lot at Children's Hospital. She killed the ignition and cut short her duet with Mary J. Blige. After she retrieved her gym bag from the backseat, Albert, the security guard, appeared out of nowhere.

"Morning, Dr. James."

Sydney grabbed her chest. "Albert, you scared the shit out of me," she said before she climbed out of the driver's seat and closed the door behind her.

"Sorry about that, Dr. James. Dr. Stevens mentioned you'd had an accident." He stepped forward to examine the damage to the hood of the vehicle. Sydney had worked at the hospital for three years and was very familiar with the security staff. When she worked overnight shifts, Albert always made sure she got to her car safely.

Sydney glanced at the speckles of dried spit on the driver's side window.

"Other than my bruised ego and being late for work, I'm fine," she answered, then rushed through the secured entrance, checking her watch as the elevator doors closed behind her. It had been almost three hours since her shift began. She exited the elevator on the fifth floor and never looked up. Her subconscious guided the way to the doctors' lounge.

Minutes later, freshly showered and ready to begin her rounds, Sydney strolled down the corridor outlined by the dark blue baseboards and nursery rhyme murals of stars, cows, and moons. She stopped at the nurses' station, but before she retrieved her clipboard, she stretched her arms above her head, twisting from side to side to relieve the tension in her middle back. Her private cell phone vibrated inside her pocket. She looked at the screen but didn't recognize the number. "Sydney James," she answered.

"Sydney, is that you, babe?" the familiar yet unidentifiable voice said anxiously. "This is your neighbor, Barbara Brown, from across the street and—"

"Mrs. Brown, is everything okay?"

A clear image of her meddlesome neighbor took shape in her mind. Sydney had been raised to respect her elders, but Mrs. Brown constantly tried her patience. If you looked up *nosy* in the dictionary, Mrs. Brown's picture would be right there.

"Hon, your house alarm went off about an hour ago, so I called the police. They're here now to check it out."

Sydney glanced at her watch.

"I told the police that you and Donathan were out of town and wouldn't be returning for a few more days, so I—"

"Mrs. Brown, we came back from Carmel last night. Donathan should be at home right now."

"Well, I told Herbert that's what I thought." Her voice trailed off as she processed what she'd just said. "But I haven't seen Donathan since you left."

Sydney shook her head in disbelief. She wasn't in the mood for a dose of Mrs. Brown and her antics today.

"Well, you gave me this number and told me to call you if there was ever a problem, and I ain't seen a hair of your husband since you left—"

"Mrs. Brown, is the alarm still going off? What is it the officers need?" Sydney struggled to keep the impatience out of her voice.

"Well, they just need to verify things are okay. I didn't want anything to happen to your house while you were away, so when I heard that alarm go off, I told Herbert I was going to call the police. I didn't want you to come home and all your belongings be gone."

Sydney rolled her eyes upward and sighed. Gone? There was no way anyone was going to get anything out of the house without Mrs. Brown seeing or hearing something. She pulled at the black elastic band that held her hair in a ponytail. It was giving her a headache.

"Mrs. Brown, thank you for looking out for us; we really appreciate it."

"Is there a number for Donathan that you want me to give to them?"

"No, ma'am. I'm going to hang up and give him a call right now."

"All right, then, suga, you do that."

Sydney ended the call and immediately dialed her home number. Donathan picked up on the first ring.

"Hey, boo," she whispered into the phone as she headed down the hallway toward the Neonatal Intensive Care Unit. "I just got off the phone with Mrs. Brown. Apparently the alarm went off about an hour ago and she called the police. They're outside responding to her call."

"I set it off when I left earlier, but the alarm company called and I took care of it. I swear, that lady has got too much time on her hands."

"I know, but at least she's watching the house."

"More like watching other folks' business." He chuckled. "I don't understand why she called the police; if she heard the alarm going off, she definitely had to hear me leave on the motorcycle. Did you get checked out yet?"

"I'm starting my rounds now, but I promise to let someone look at me soon."

"You know, you could come back home and I'd be happy to check you out thoroughly myself."

"Don't tempt me."

"Well, I guess I'll have to wait until tonight to do my inspection."

Sydney giggled.

"All right, babe. I'm on my way out to talk to the men in blue."

After saying good-bye a second time, Sydney hurried down the hall and bumped into Dr. Day exiting the double doors that led to the NICU. Miles was new to the neurosurgery team at Children's, having only been at the hospital for two months. In that short time he'd had the female nurses taking bets on which one was going to run her fingers through the perfect-sized dreadlocks that rested neatly at the nape of his neck and which one was going to get in his bed first.

"You're definitely a sight for tired eyes," he said warmly. She flashed him a brilliant smile in return.

His six-foot-four, lean, muscular frame towered over her. He was already dressed in street clothes beneath his lab coat—a Ralph Lauren black T-shirt with its signature red polo horse and expensive black slacks tailored to fall just above his Gucci sneakers. She tracked his eyes as they fastened on the V-neck of her scrubs, skimmed her entire body, then took a slow return trip back to her face. Instinctively, Sydney drew her hand to the bruise across her chest.

"I appreciate you covering for me."

"If the tables were turned, I'm sure you would have done the same." His eyes focused on the bruise. "Are you okay?"

"My collarbone is a little tender. When I get a chance, I'll run down to the imaging department and have someone take an X-ray."

"Would you like me to cover for you a little while longer so you can take care of that?"

"No. I've kept you here long enough. I'll wait until things settle down a bit, then get someone to take care of it. So, what did I miss?"

"A baby girl, last name Perkins, born with spina bifida. Birth by C-section, near full term, but she weighed four pounds, one ounce. She was transported here by helicopter from John Muir Medical Center in Walnut Creek. The opening level was an approximate L1 and as you know that means complete lower body paralysis and no control of bowl and bladder functions. The long-term prognosis doesn't look good," Miles recited.

"Have you spoken with the parents yet?"

"The mother is still hospitalized at John Muir. There was no mention of a father. The baby arrived alone."

Sydney felt a sudden sadness. As a pediatric neurosurgeon, having to be the one who shattered parents' dreams for their children was the most difficult part of her job. She couldn't imagine being a mother—especially a single mother—learning that her child would face lifelong medical challenges and being helpless to do anything about it. She forced a smile and changed the subject. "How about I buy you an early lunch?"

A coy smile played at the corners of his mouth. "Food sounds wonderful, but I'll have to take a rain check. I was just about to cancel my Comcast installation for this afternoon, but since you're here, I think I can still make it to my loft in time for the appointment. I've watched the *Love Jones* and *Boomerang* DVDs so much in the last two months I know every single word, and that's scary." They laughed in unison.

"A rain check it is, then. Maybe we can go someplace other than the hospital cafeteria and I can bring along my girlfriend, Payton."

Sydney watched Miles closely as he smothered a groan and shook his head. He'd transferred here from Chicago, and she guessed his reaction was related to the residual effects of other staff members trying to make love connections for him. Miles certainly didn't look like he needed any help in that department.

"I think you'd like her."

Miles lowered his head; a hint of a smile exposing his dimples.

"She's a very attractive woman," Sydney said convincingly.

He held the door to the NICU open, making room for Sydney to pass under his makeshift bridge. Their pagers went off in unison.

He spoke first. "It's probably the Perkins baby. C'mon, I'll help you get started."

Sydney shook her head. "Miles, you go home. You've already been here for sixteen hours and you look exhausted. If I need an extra hand, Julia can help me."

Miles clipped his pager back onto his belt. "I really don't mind."

"Didn't you just say you had a Comcast appointment to keep?"

Miles nodded and smiled. "Yeah, I did. But call me if you need me," he said, before he turned on his heel and disappeared down the corridor.

As the double doors of the NICU closed behind her, Sydney found herself bombarded with the synchronized sounds of mechanical breathing. The space was large, with a circular nurses' station situated in the middle of the room. Multicolored lifelines attached to the tiny incubators were visible, and regulated beeps filled the room. Her eyes locked on a young couple standing over a tiny infant lying on her back. The child was motionless; a girl she guessed by the pink cap that rested beside her in the clear bassinette. Her head was wrapped snuggly with gauze to stabilize the IV inserted in the vein that ran down the front of her forehead. The mother was on one side, gently brushing her finger along the side of the baby's cheek, the father on the other, resting his index finger in the baby's tiny palm. Sydney felt sad. Most of the babies in NICU had somebody who cared about them, but there were others who hadn't been touched or held by anyone other than doctors and nurses in weeks.

"Over here, Dr. James," one of the nurses called, seizing her attention.

Sydney made her way across the aisle, gazed down at the baby, and sighed before removing the stethoscope from her coat pocket. She hoped there was something she could do to make life more bearable for the baby, even if it was only for a little while.

Chapter 3

Sydney drove from Children's Hospital to her home in the El Cerrito Hills in record time. It was almost eight in the evening, but daylight savings time had been in effect for a few weeks and there was still daylight. She felt like every nerve ending along her neck and shoulders had a ton of bricks sitting on them. Between cases, she'd gone to the X-ray department for pictures of her neck and shoulder. The diagnosis was nothing more than some ibuprofen, a hot bubble bath, and a glass of wine couldn't cure.

Sydney sighed heavily as she turned her Range Rover on to Terrace Drive. She was glad this day was almost over and happy to finally be home. Idling in front of her driveway, she waited for the wrought-iron gate to slide open. She heard her name being called in the distance.

"Sydney, Sydney, baby."

In her rearview mirror, she saw her neighbor, Barbara Brown, carefully stepping down the straight flight of stairs that led from the street to her front door, carrying something. Sydney's face warmed with annoyance; the words *I don't need this right now* echoed in her head.

Engine still running, Sydney took her time getting out of the car. She was tired and the last thing she felt like doing was listening to Mrs. Brown ramble on about the neighborhood gossip. Hearsay was her specialty, and Sydney knew that was exactly what she'd do. The older woman, who had naturally wide eyes that made her look as if she was always surprised about something, approached her wearing a pale yellow housedress with an apron secured tightly around her waist. She was carrying a pie, which she handed to Sydney.

"Baby, are you all right? That truck of yours looks like you've been in a car fight, and it don't look like you won the altercation." She craned her head around Sydney to get a better look at the Range Rover.

Sydney blew out a haggard breath and shifted her weight from one foot to the other; the warm dish melted away her annoyance. The aroma of Barbara Brown's purple sweet potato pie enticed Sydney to shed her impatience and be more cordial to her neighbor.

"No, ma'am; I was in an accident this morning, I have a splitting headache and all I want to do is lay down."

"Oh, honey, I'm so sorry to hear that. I want to apologize to you again about calling the police this morning," Barbara Brown said, rubbing her hand up and down Sydney's arm. "Your alarm was screaming like a newborn baby and I just didn't know what to do. I was afraid a couple of those thieving rascals don' snuck up in there and was takin' ya stuff."

Although Sydney's head continued to throb, a slight smile turned her lips upward. Barbara Brown really did mean well and there *had* been a few burglaries on the street. Sydney was grateful she not only had a state-of-the-art alarm system to protect her home but also the best neighborhood watch lady in the country. At least Mrs. Brown's nosiness was good for something.

"It wasn't a problem, Mrs. Brown, and I want you to know that Donathan and I both appreciate you looking out for us."

"Oh, baby, I don't mind. It's no trouble at all," she said, embracing Sydney in a hug that lingered uncomfortably long. She stepped back and released Sydney from her grasp. "Well, get you some rest, suga. I got to get back to my baking for the church auxiliary. Enjoy the pie."

Sydney briefly watched as Barbara Brown ascended the stairs a lot quicker than she'd come down them. Once she disappeared into the house, Sydney returned to her car and drove through the gate.

When she entered the front door, a whiff of grilled salmon aroused her senses. "Donathan," she called before she rested her tote bag on the entry table and hung her jacket on the coatrack affixed to the inside of the foyer closet door.

"In here, babe," he called as she moved toward the kitchen and the wonderful smell.

Donathan was standing over their Wolf stove, barefoot, in jeans and a T-shirt, with a kitchen towel draped over his shoulder. She placed the pie dish on the granite countertop, her eyes lingering on his smooth, milk-chocolate skin. This morning he'd had the three-day stubble she was so fond of, especially when it tickled the insides of her thighs, but now he was clean-shaven except for the neatly trimmed goatee. He reminded her of a mature Lance Gross. He looked up and smiled, his dark brown eyes closing almost to slits.

"Come here and taste this," he said, summoning her to the raised spoon, his hand acting as a ladle to catch any overflow.

"How did you know I was starving?" she asked, blowing on the spoon before taking a bite. "Ummm." She inhaled, closed her eyes, and dropped her head back as the food danced across her palate.

"'Cause it's my job to know," he said, backing her into the countertop, kissing her gently on her neck. Her body stiffened. Donathan raised his head, making uncompromising eye contact with her. There was no mistaking the question in his stare.

"Yes, I got X-rayed; nothing is fractured, just bruising and muscle strain."

"Good girl." He rested his hands on her hips. "Why don't you go take a hot bath, and by the time you finish, dinner will be ready?"

"But I'm hungry now, boo." She pouted.

"I know, but the pasta needs to boil for a few more minutes

and I need to finish making the salad." He took a sip of Chardonnay, then handed his wineglass to her. "Take this and go," he said, then playfully patted her behind and shooed her out of the kitchen. "I need about twenty more minutes."

After Sydney climbed the stairs and entered the bathroom, a shower was all she could muster. The rhythmic droplets of hot water massaged her aching body and made her forget about the day's events. Afterward, she dried and oiled her body, wrapped herself in a towel, then made her way through the vanity area, headed toward her bed, with the intention of resting her eyes for a minute.

A wide grin spread across her face when she noticed a few surprises on her nightstand—two gift boxes covered in black satin and organza ribbon and a black envelope propped against another glass of wine. Without a second thought, she hurried over and tore open the envelope.

Do you like champagne? Put on the items from the boxes, drink your glass of wine, then slip on the blindfold and wait for me . . .

Within a few seconds, she'd found a champagne-colored Millesia Diablesse silk demi-cup bra with raised embroidery, a matching thong panty, and a pair of Christian Louboutin patent-leather pumps.

"Good choice," she purred, admiring the color of the lingerie. It reminded her of the nail polish on her toes: chocolate frost, her favorite, the one she picked on most visits to the nail salon.

Donathan had a thing for expensive lingerie and shoes and she had an extensive lingerie and shoe collection to prove it. His one requisite: that she wore them for the first time for him. He had told her on many occasions that silks, satins, and embroidered laces next to her skin got his dick hard and she could definitely understand why he liked the combination.

Before stepping into the thong, Sydney rushed into the bathroom to quickly wash up. Her breathing slowed at the feel of the silk against her skin. She admired the satin ties that rested on her hips, then placed her arms through the two-stranded bra straps and hooked the front clasp between her breasts. She glided her oiled feet into the four-inch pumps and fell back onto the bed, the 1000-thread-count sheets pressed against her back. Everything felt so good, so smooth, and so cool. With the blindfold twisted between her fingertips, she closed her eyes for what seemed like only a moment and opened them to the sound of Donathan placing a serving tray on the nightstand. Her lashes fluttered as she struggled to keep her eyes open. He picked up her wineglass and looked intently at her.

"You look beautiful," Donathan said, marveling, his voice husky and low.

"Thanks, baby," she said, her eyes now wide open and taking in the full view of her handsome husband. She loved the way he looked at her. He sat down on the bed beside her, balanced the wineglass in his left hand, and traced circles around her erect nipples with his right.

Sydney felt his finger rest a moment on the bra closure between her breasts, then with a feathery stroke he drew a curvy line downward toward the triangle of champagne fabric peeking from between her legs. Her breath caught in her stomach as he moved his finger further south, maneuvered her panty to the side, and started fingering her. Sydney moaned as he dipped his finger in and out of her wetness.

"So wet," he whispered. "I can't wait to taste you."

"I can't wait for you to taste me either," she responded as she scooted to the center of the bed.

Donathan continued his gentle assault, the silence in the room broken only by her oohs and aahs. He licked his way down and then up again, taking his time before he unhooked her bra and released her perfect D cups in the process. She untangled her arms from the straps, then welcomed Donathan's wet, sultry kisses on her erect nipples, which sent jolts of pleasure cascading through her body. Now on his knees, positioned between her legs, he pulled his T-shirt over his head, his muscular biceps flexing, then removed her panty and planted a trail of butterfly kisses that made her stomach flutter. First he nibbled and licked, then tasted Sydney, masterfully exploring the wetness between her thighs until she ached. Sydney rhythmically chased the euphoric sensations, begging him not to stop. "Oh, baby, that feels so good," she murmured. "Right there . . ."

With the signature red-soled shoes crisscrossed behind his shoulders, Sydney thrust her hips toward the heat that lingered on the tip of Donathan's talented tongue as it pushed her over the edge.

"Oh . . . God . . . fuck . . . oh . . . God." She melted into the all-consuming, orgasmic wave that crashed through her body. She basked in the sensations for a moment, her calls to God and earthy words becoming whispers, leaving her glowing all over. Satisfied, she rolled away from him and pushed herself up on his side of the bed and pulled the sheets across her nakedness to ward off a chill.

Donathan laughed. "Don't cover up on my account."

He fluffed the huge pillows that rested against the headboard, patting them with his hands.

"Sit right here, baby, so I can feed you."

Sydney languished among the pillows and Donathan carefully placed the tray on her lap. She made a wry face as she noticed the tray held only one plate of food.

"Honey, where's your plate so we can feed each other?"

As he filled the fork with a bite of food, Sydney opened her mouth, then closed her lips around the angel-hair pasta. He paused for a moment, held her gaze, and said, "I've already had my dinner."

Chapter 4

Rattled by the loud ringing of her phone, Sydney sat up in bed, disoriented, before she grabbed the screaming device off the receiver.

"Hello," she grumbled, glancing at the clock that said it was one in the afternoon. Usually her alarm woke her up at five a.m., but it hadn't today. It was Saturday, she was off work, and all she wanted to do was lay in her bed for as long as she felt like it.

"Please tell me you are *not* still sleeping," Payton stated.

Sydney covered her face with a pillow and sighed heavily. She was so exhausted; she'd forgotten they were going shopping.

"Get your ass up," Payton yelled into the phone. "I'm driving up Moeser Lane and I'll be there in five minutes—"

Sydney tossed the pillow off her face and jumped out of bed, still a little sore from the accident yesterday. "You're where? Why did you wait until you were almost here to call me? I need to shower and get dressed."

"Girl, if I'd called you when I was still on Highway 4, you and I both know you would have stayed in bed until I arrived at your front door. Now get off the phone because I'll be there in a few minutes."

Phone back on the receiver, Sydney headed toward the master bathroom, hoping a quick hot shower would ease her discomfort.

★ ★ ★

The afternoon traffic was slow as Payton Janelle Jones took the Cutting Boulevard exit. An advertisement for PerfectChemistry.com, an internet dating service, blared from the radio, and she paused for a moment, shuddering at the memory of her morning breakfast date. That had to have been the longest hour of her life. There was no way she would ever let a fat fuck like that touch her. His roaming eyes had been all over her body, fondling her as if she were a piece of meat. She'd be so happy when she was done trolling for men on the internet.

Dating married men wasn't a problem for Payton, but it was a problem for Sydney, who'd talked her into using an internet dating service in the first place. For Payton, married men with wives who didn't understand them represented a clichéd and delicate situation; a problem if you were the wife, but it worked out beautifully for Payton. She'd heard all the classic reasons men strayed—the wives weren't fucking; they would have left a long time ago if it weren't for the kids—but she didn't believe one word of that bullshit.

Deep down, she knew why these quasi-relationships appealed to her. There was no long-term commitment, the men played by her rules, and she got to fuck whoever she wanted.

Because Payton was playing the chauffeur, Sydney felt she should at least make an effort and go shopping. She stood outside her front door dressed in a chocolate-brown velour sweat suit with a Gucci messenger bag anchored across her left shoulder. Jackie O–style sunglasses framed her makeup-free face. As the gate parted like the Red Sea for the Lexus LS600, it occurred to her that she really did have a legitimate reason to cancel this outing. But before she could formulate it into an articulate persuasion, the car had stopped in front of her and she was in the front seat scowling as Payton, with the enthusiasm of a new puppy, gave her details of their itinerary.

"I need to go to Saks and Neiman's, then we can go to Crustacean for a late lunch."

Sydney stared at her friend. Payton was beautiful—her brown eyes and perfect white teeth playing center stage to a contagious Colgate smile that grabbed a hold of you and wouldn't let go. She sat in the driver's seat, holding her smile, the corners of her mouth stretched like a Cheshire cat's. "So what happened yesterday?" Payton asked as they drove down San Pablo, heading toward the freeway. "I spoke with Donathan briefly this morning before my breakfast date."

"That was your behind calling so early this morning?" Sydney frowned. She and Payton usually talked on the phone at least once a day, but yesterday had been so hectic, they'd missed each other. And she'd forgotten all about the breakfast date.

She immediately started in with the questions. "Well?"

"Well, what?" Payton responded, glancing over at her.

"The date. Tell me what happened."

"Where do you want me to begin?" she asked dryly.

"How about eight o'clock this morning?"

Payton sneered like she was reliving the experience, then said, "Internet dating is not for me. I don't care if I see another fake dating profile as long as I live. And the sex was horrible."

Sydney frowned, disturbed by her friend's confession.

"That nasty troll this morning topped the cake. He was worse than the others—definitely no love connection."

"I thought this internet dating was an opportunity for you to find a nice guy of your own. Not to add more men to your list. I hope you're at least practicing safe sex," Sydney said, removing her sunglasses and staring at Payton.

Payton was quiet and looked straight ahead as they merged onto Interstate 80. "Well, it was about meeting a nice guy and I didn't, but I did complete the required six dates and now I'm eligible to get my money back. At least I tried."

Sydney stared in disbelief. "You are, aren't you?" she questioned, the pitch of her voice escalating.

"Of course I practiced safe sex, I'm not stupid. Although I did have a little problem with Isaiah, the second match," she said, glancing at Sydney out of the corner of her eye and holding up her right hand to show a three-inch width with her thumb and pointer finger. "Have you ever run across a fine-ass man with a small dick? I tried everything. I kissed it, licked it, and blew on it, but nothing helped. It felt like he was tickling me at first, then it turned into serious friction. I had to go to the doctor behind that foolishness—"

"Oh, God," Sydney mumbled. She couldn't believe what she was hearing. "The doctor? What for?"

"Too much friction."

Sydney sighed. She had known Payton for almost twenty years, but it still amazed her how reckless Payton was when it came to sex.

"You didn't use any lubricant?"

"Well, normally I don't need lubricant."

"Girl, you are too damn old to be letting a man screw you without lubricant. So what did the doctor say?"

"She told me I needed to use lubricant," Payton responded, nearly laughing out loud again.

"I'm scared to ask you for the details of what happened this morning."

"Now that shit was crazy. My PerfectChemistry match, Lloyd, works nights at the Oakland Airport, so I agreed to meet him at Denny's on Hegenberger. I arrived first and was seated, and girl, I almost lost it when this short man with a serious beer gut playing hide and seek with his belt walked toward my booth, smiling. It took everything in me to sit through a meal with that man."

Sydney closed her eyes and shook her head.

"His breath was so bad I had to run back home to change my blouse before I headed out to Pittsburg. The smell had seeped into my clothing."

"Ooo, that sounds nasty."

"You haven't heard nasty. Just before we left Denny's, he excused himself to the restroom and came back with a wet spot on the front of his pants."

"Damn," Sydney said, laughing. Maybe this internet dating wasn't such a good idea for Payton after all, but she had just the solution. "Hey, do you remember Miles, the neurosurgeon I've been telling you about from work?"

Payton shook her head.

"C'mon, Payton, I owe him lunch and I told him I'd bring you along."

"Sydney, I am so done with letting you have anything to do with finding me a man. If it weren't for you and your matchmaking ideas, I'd have more money in my purse right now to spend on this shopping excursion."

Sydney looked out the window as they approached the toll station on the San Francisco Bay Bridge. She looked over at Payton, who, underneath the protective armor of her designer attire and flawless makeup, looked lonely. In all the years she'd known Payton, Sydney couldn't remember her having a relationship with a man for more than six months. Sydney reached across the console and gently touched Payton's hand.

"Payton, why do you feel the need to copulate with people you barely know?"

Payton froze, as if the words had stung her, but quickly rebounded and sighed impatiently. She drew back her hand to count four one-dollar bills, paid the toll, and waited for the metering light in her lane to turn green.

"For one, I enjoy sex, and two, if I was a man, you wouldn't be asking me that question, and third, not everybody is perfect like you."

Sydney glanced out the window, wondering what Payton meant by that comment. She certainly wasn't perfect and she *definitely* liked sex. She just liked sex with her husband and not with every Tom, Dick, and Harry of the male persuasion. It was the trust and intimacy she shared with her husband that gave her the freedom to do anything she wanted in the bedroom, and she couldn't think of letting another man touch her. For Payton, different men and casual sex was a way of life—like the air she breathed. But how long did Payton think she could run around like she was living in the era of free love without consequences? Albeit good or bad, everything she did in life had consequences.

Chapter 5

While Donathan James waited for his friends, Tony and Tyrese, to arrive, he walked into the private lounge of the Richmond Country Club. It was twelve noon, thirty minutes before their standing tee time. He took a seat at the bar, using the extra minutes to collect his thoughts. He looked into the crowd, at no one in particular. The country club's members were mostly businessmen and professionals from the I-80 corridor who appreciated the exclusivity of playing at a private course, but in recent months, membership to the club had become the *it* thing for up-and-coming African American professionals.

Today, women, mostly in pairs, seemed to be there to take full advantage of the amenities the club had to offer. Specifically, they sought sugar daddies, who in most cases were married but willing to accept what the ladies were offering. Sex with a price tag.

Almost everyone in the room knew Donathan; he could thank his radio show's aggressive morning marketing campaign for that. He was every woman's dream. Tall, handsome, charismatic, and he knew a thing or two about sexually pleasing a woman.

He perused the crowded dining room, taking in the imposing self-importance that existed in this newfound social setting. He spotted a woman sitting alone at a small table next to the window. She was in her early thirties, with average looks at best, but the long red nails extending from her fingertips and the reddish-brown wavy hair that rested to the middle of her back caught his attention. Donathan smirked and shook his head. He'd learned a long time ago that women who wore other people's hair and nails equaled high maintenance, and he preferred his women more attached to their natural, God-given attributes. He was forty-three years old and still hadn't figured out what made women go through so much trouble to present a false package because, in the end, nakedness hid nothing.

"What can I get for you today, Dr. James?" the bartender asked. The sleeves of his white polo shirt squeezed his biceps as he placed a coaster with a script letter *R* and crisscrossed golf clubs in front of Donathan. He glanced at his watch, then back to the bartender, whose blue eyes and tousled hair reminded him of a young Brad Pitt.

"Give me a Heineken."

"One Heineken coming right up."

It was the absentminded massaging of the diamond-studded, platinum wedding band on his ring finger that stole his smile and diverted his consciousness back to the day before. The panic in Sydney's voice had stayed with him ever since he'd gotten her call. He'd been afraid he wouldn't make it to her in time. His erratic thoughts had spun like the wheels on his motorcycle as he wove in and out of traffic to get to her. It had taken him twenty-five minutes. Good thing the police got to the scene before he did, because he was ready to strangle the bastard, who was being pushed into the backseat of the police car. What kind of man would he be if he'd let someone physically harm his wife?

As a doctor of clinical psychology, he spent most of his time trying to convince his patients they weren't crazy. When the truth of the matter was, everyone was a little crazy—just in need of the right catalyst to push them over the edge.

The bartender returned with his Heineken, and Donathan closed his eyes and took a swig of his beer, propelling the troubling thoughts from his head. "Is this seat taken?"

A curvaceous young woman stood next to him. He leaned back on the leather swivel stool and studied her for a moment. Nice legs, big breasts—she oozed sex. Just the way he liked them. Her cinnamon-brown hair was pulled back off her flawless face and large-framed sunglasses concealed her eyes.

While he pondered, she took the seat next to him and ordered a dirty martini, then adjusted herself on the stool, brushing her bare thigh against his.

"Yeah, it's taken."

She'd been fishing around inside a little red patent-leather clutch purse, but now she stopped cold.

"Oh, I'm sorry—"

"No." He smiled wickedly. "I meant it was taken by you."

"Cute," she said, removing her sunglasses and extending her manicured hand in his direction. "I'm Austyn Greene."

He gently shook her hand and then took another swig of his beer, willing his eyes not to look down at her overabundant cleavage. Out of all the empty seats, she had to choose this one. At first glance she was no different from all the other women who tried to pick him up. But at closer inspection her exotic features and pouty lips wouldn't be easily forgotten, nor would the restlessness and sadness behind her eyes, which betrayed her sexy demeanor. She pulled out a twenty-dollar bill, placed it on the counter, and swiveled on her stool. Their knees touched.

"Ouch," she purred, reaching for her knee. "I think I need a doctor."

From the moment he'd sat down, he'd known it wouldn't be long before someone approached him for advice or an autograph. *The Sex Doctor*—his face was plastered all over the Bay Area on billboards, and he couldn't go anywhere without people recognizing him. His radio persona had created fertile opportunities for trouble, like the kind that'd just sat down next to him. He cleared his throat and hoped she was a fan rather than the paparazzi.

"A doctor? What makes you think I'm a doctor?" he asked, lowering his shades, his dark brown eyes giving her a stony stare.

"You are the doctor who specializes in the art of sex, right? The one from the morning radio show. I've tried to call in so we could discuss my issue, but I can never seem to get through."

He chuckled. "Well, nobody has ever referred to what I do on the radio as art. After all, I'm just a therapist who talks to people about their sexual issues live on the radio."

"Exactly," she said and downed her martini in three fast gulps and signaled to the bartender for a second. "Now, can I persuade you to give me a private session?"

Donathan said nothing; instead, he took another swig of his beer. In situations like these, he found it best to let the women talk. Then he'd find out exactly what they wanted.

"I see you staring at me." She giggled, tilting her head back, her laughter sending waves through her bosom. "Are you a breast man? Because I've imagined that you are."

He grinned. "We're here now, so why don't you tell me about your issues—"

"Are you really a doctor?" Austyn asked, switching from her role as sex kitten to sounding sincerely interested.

Donathan nodded. To his mother's chagrin, he was a PhD doctor, not a medical doctor, but that was none of Austyn Greene's business. She scooted to the edge of her seat and faced him.

"I get off listening to you on the radio. Your deep baritone voice advising people on how to deal with their sexual issues. Ummm," she purred, closing her eyes, moaning like he was touching her.

Donathan jumped as a firm hand gripped his left shoulder.

"I knew I'd find you in here," Tony said, scrutinizing the woman sitting next to his friend. Donathan stood, reached for his wallet, and placed a crisp twenty-dollar bill on the bar.

"I was wondering where you guys were." He stuttered like a kid who'd been caught with his hand in the candy jar.

"We've been waiting in the cart-holding area," Tony said, shooting Austyn a look of disdain. "I'll meet you outside."

Donathan turned back to Austyn and extended his hand.

"It was a pleasure meeting you," he said, then turned toward the exit.

"Wait!" she called after him, reaching out to grab his arm. He jerked away automatically, sensing this was some kind of game for her. It seemed she had arrived at the bar with every intention of luring him in. "What about my issue?" she managed in a desperate tone.

He stopped in midstride and turned back to face her, weighing his options. He'd already decided this chick was a whack job, but he was curious nonetheless. "Look, Austyn," he said, feeling awkward, "I'd like to help you, but here's the thing: This isn't the time or place. Why don't you call in to the radio station and tell them I said to put you through? We can talk about it then."

"No worries," she said with an airy wave of her hand. "I'm sure we'll have another opportunity to talk about it soon."

Donathan smiled, backed away, then turned to catch up with Tony, who was holding the door open for him, his face stern. Donathan gave him a quick once-over, noticing his eyes were missing their usual luster. His six-foot-three frame looked leaner today.

"Is it just me or was that some weird shit I just walked up on?" Tony asked as he and Donathan headed toward Tyrese and the waiting golf cart.

He smiled at the thought of the sexy woman masturbating to his voice as it blared through her radio. "I'd have to agree with you on that one, man," Donathan said as he grabbed his clubs from the holding area and placed them in the rear of the cart. He jumped in the second row of seats, behind his friends.

"I can't remember the last time both of you were on time. Am I on *Punk'd* or something?" he asked, laughing.

Two hours later and well into their back nine, Donathan leaned against the cart, enjoying the rolling green hills and the view of the Golden Gate Bridge. It was beautiful out here, but it was only April and the sweat was pouring down his back like a waterfall. He took a momentary look at his friends.

"Damn, it's hot out here. We're going to have to tee off a little earlier," he said, using the small towel tucked in his waistband to dab the sweat off his brow.

"How's Sydney?" Tony asked, preparing to take his swing. Donathan had left him and Tyrese both a message about the accident the day before.

"She's fine, out spending money with Payton, but her truck is fucked up. I had it towed to Cole European this morning."

Tyrese shook his head, his six-foot-seven frame towering over everyone. He removed his hat, exposing his already bronze bald head, then used his forearm to wipe the sweat from his brow. "People are crazy nowadays. You never know when they're going to pull out a gun over a fender bender. I mean, what's the point? It's just a car."

"Exactly, but I'm glad the police got there before I did."

"Shit, I'm glad that wasn't Joi," Tyrese said. "Her ass probably would have been the one hitting somebody's car with a shovel."

They all laughed.

"This morning, while I was getting dressed, I kept hearing a beeping noise that ended up being a voice-activated digital recorder that Joi had taped underneath the bed. It had been taping my telephone conversations."

"Nothing incriminating, I hope?" Donathan said, stepping forward and readying for the game-ending swing. "Did you confront Joi about it?"

"I did, but her response was, 'It must have been the boys playing around.'"

Tony, now sitting in the front seat of the golf cart, tugged at the bib of his white cap and looked at Tyrese with a rigid stare.

"Man, you should be concerned. Your twins are four years old, and I'm not saying they're not smart, but what does a four-year-old know about a digital recorder? The fact that your wife went to those lengths says a lot about what she's willing to do. Both you and Donathan need to cut out that creeping mess before somebody gets hurt."

Tyrese looked up, his piercing gray eyes focused on Tony. "Joi's harmless. Before I left home, I gave her some good loving, and when I left the house, she was purring and asking me what I wanted for dinner."

"So, are you still coming to Maxwell's tonight?" Donathan asked, recognizing a need to change the subject.

"Man, I needed a get-out-of-jail card, so I promised Joi that I would take her and the boys to the movies." Tyrese steered the cart back into the return area, then checked his watch. "Shit, I'm about to be late."

"You need to cover your tracks better," Donathan called after him. "The last thing you need to do is fuel a suspicious wife."

"I got this," he said, hurrying toward his truck. "I'll holla at y'all later."

Donathan turned to Tony. "What about you?" he said, eyeing his friend with worry. He looked exhausted, but maybe a night out would recharge his battery.

"I think I'm staying in tonight. I picked up my aunt Rosemary from the airport yesterday, so maybe tonight I'll be able to get me some rest."

"Good. You look like you need it. How's Moms doing?"

"She's good."

"Well, call me later if you change your mind."

After watching Tony leave, Donathan approached his own car, where he found a business card with a lipstick kiss tucked into the weather stripping on the driver's side door. He read the message, then flipped the card over and studied the East Bay telephone number. She was so fucking sexy.

Her handwritten message said to call her so they could discuss her issues, but if he did, he had a feeling her issues wouldn't be the only thing they'd discuss. *Should he? Shouldn't he?* he pondered, remembering those unforgettable pouty lips. His gut instinct told him she was young and probably immature, which meant drama. And he despised drama.

Problem solved, he thought as he tucked the card in his front pocket and made a mental note to pass it along to his producers. He honestly didn't know if she deserved it, but Austyn Greene had just earned herself a spot on the *never*-put-through list.

Chapter 6

Payton stepped out of the shower. She couldn't remember the last time she'd been this giddy about any man. There was something deliciously wicked about keeping a secret...like the one she and Tony were keeping. They'd been fucking for three months now, and both Donathan and Sydney were none the wiser.

Tony called and, to her surprise, agreed to come over, which was something he'd never done. They always played on his turf, which was fine with her. But since he'd recently moved his sister and his terminally ill mother into the house with him, their East Oakland rendezvous was no longer an option.

Cupping her breasts, she turned slightly and stared in silence at her perfect, round, chocolate ass, and, unlike her need to keep everyone in her life at arm's length, this was one of the better attributes given to her by her mother.

Shutting off the bathroom light, she passed down a short hall and stepped into her walk-in closet, in search of something to put on. She shimmied into her black lace boy shorts and matching racer-back lace tee, deep in thought about how Sydney had questioned her about her need for sex today. She couldn't stop thinking about it and it didn't make sense. Why did she care? When it came to sex, Sydney was a prude, a fucking nun, and she didn't have a clue about sexual freedom. But still, Payton resented being judged by her. She surveyed her image in the full-length mirror.

"Damn, I look so good, I'd fuck me."

Once in her bedroom, she heard her cell phone humming on the nightstand, and she picked it up without looking at the caller ID. "Hello."

"Little girl, who gave you the right to sell my daddy's house?" shouted a familiar voice through the phone. Payton shook her head and sighed. It was her uncle Sheldon. She had known he would call sooner or later. Earlier in the day, she'd met with a real estate investor who had agreed to buy her grandparents' house.

"Uncle Sheldon, I told you things were going to change."

"Where am I supposed to go, Payton?"

"How about rehab, for starters?" she snapped.

Sheldon Jones was sixty-two years old, and he was the reason Payton found herself running back and forth to Pittsburg every week to manage one crisis after another.

"C'mon, Niecy," he begged, using the name he affectionately called her. She took a long, deep breath and shifted her weight from one foot to the other, a bit agitated.

"I know this decision is a hard one, but I think it's best for everybody—"

"Everybody? Meaning you," he exploded. "I bet my daddy is turning over in his grave. You know he didn't want you to sell his house."

"He didn't want you smoking crack either, did he?" she spat back.

"Niecy, I promise this time it's gon' be different. I'll get a job and pay the taxes and insurance."

Payton held the phone away from her ear while her uncle rambled on. There was nothing new about what he was saying. She'd heard his song and dance before and she'd made up her mind. This time there was no turning back.

Just as she was thinking this, her intercom buzzed from downstairs, letting her know her guest had arrived.

"Uncle Sheldon, I have to go. I'll give you a call tomorrow; we can talk more about this then." Payton ended the call and held the red button until the cell phone powered off because she knew he'd call right back. She stood still for a few moments, contemplating her decision. If everything went according to plan, for the first time since her grandfather's death and being named the executor of his estate, she would no longer be responsible for her uncles Sheldon and Donald—two grown-ass men—and she couldn't wait.

The moment the door opened, she threw herself at him, wrapping her long, bare legs around his waist, kissing him hard, her tongue darting in and out of his mouth.

"Looks like someone isn't in the mood for conversation tonight," Tony said, his smile a little less enthusiastic than usual. He was an average-looking man, but when he walked into a room, women took notice. His mysterious eyes, meticulous style, and confidence drove women crazy.

"I was about to fix myself a cocktail. Would you like one?"

He brushed the black lace stretched across her pert nipples. "What are my choices?"

"Beer, wine, gin, gin," she repeated, her voice trailing off as she unwrapped herself and headed toward the bar. When he didn't answer immediately, she looked over her shoulder and found him staring at her ass. She tossed him a knowing look.

"I'll take the gin."

Payton slid behind the bar and Tony took a seat on one of the stools. She poured herself a glass of wine and mixed up a Bombay Sapphire Salty Dog, Tony's drink of choice. She stirred the contents with her finger as he opened his mouth and sucked it in greedily to sample the concoction.

"How's that?"

"Perfect."

Tony followed Payton into the bedroom, walked over to the floor-to-ceiling window, and stared out over Lake Merritt. The lake was lined with thousands of white lights that reflected off the water, and the illumination of the Henry J. Kaiser Center made the view majestic.

"The lake looks much better from up here," he said, taking a sip from the salt-rimmed glass, his back to her.

"Take your clothes off."

He turned around, a wicked look in his eyes. "Oh, so now we're exhibitionists," he said, gesturing toward the floor-to-ceiling windows.

"I do have a little exhibitionism in my blood, but if you must know, the windows have a special coating that allows me and you to see out but prevents others from seeing in."

"Sounds kinky."

"Hold that thought," Payton said, scurrying toward the bathroom. She turned on the shower and adjusted the water pressure to a hard pulse. She was horny and ready to explore without inhibitions, and that always required her partners to shower first. She laid out fresh towels, picked up her wineglass, and moved back through the bedroom, where Tony had begun undressing.

"I'm going to freshen up my drink. Do you want some more sin?" she said, making a reference to the cliché that gin will make you sin, and he laughed out loud because he knew exactly what she was talking about.

"Of course."

A few minutes later she returned to the bedroom, her glass of red wine in one hand and his elixir in the other. The shower was still running. She placed his new drink on the granite nightstand closest to the bathroom, then took another gulp from her glass of wine, feeling the tingles in her extremities and the wetness stirring between her legs. She opened the top drawer and removed a palm sized object from a slender leather pouch. She pushed the power button, the soft hum emitting from the silicone vibrating tip growing stronger, until she felt the speed and intensity she wanted pulsating in her hand.

She turned down her Egyptian cotton satin sheets and climbed into the bed, her vibrating apparatus in tow. She closed her eyes and leaned back into the sea of pillows, imagining Tony brushing the creamy white towel across his rock-hard body, a direct benefit of his jumping on and off a big brown UPS truck, delivering boxes and packages all day. She opened her legs and dangled the pulsating ball across her center; a soft moan escaped her lips. She reached into her lace panties and touched herself, her senses heightened.

Tony cleared his throat and leaned against the doorframe, the towel wrapped casually around his waist. Payton made eye contact and grinned.

"Looks like you started without me, but don't stop," he said. "I'm enjoying the show."

Payton closed her eyes but felt him fixated, watching her. She imagined his eyes were his hands and she could feel them exploring her body.

He finished his drink and climbed onto the bed beside her. He smelled good, and that was a turn-on. He lightly stroked her hair, his eyes fixed on her breasts, each breath she took lifting them toward him. Barely making contact, his fingertips approached her nipples. Payton shuddered, moved her hips faster, and melted into her perfect rhythm. He lifted her lace T-shirt and gauged her response as he made small circles around the swollen cinnamon flesh.

"You're beautiful," he whispered, kissing her neck gently. His tongue lingered at the curve of her shoulder, sending jolts of excitement through her body. She was on fire.

His middle finger inched slowly, found its way, and slid into her center. Payton paused momentarily and then fucked his finger, her moans giving voice to her intensifying excitement. She could feel his stiff dick brushing against her thigh. Her pussy tightened, pulsating around his finger.

"You starting without me?" he said, his voice low and deep. He pushed in another finger deeper and a tormented expression washed across her face.

"Is that what you want?"

Payton panted, breathing heavily, on the verge of nirvana. "I-want-it," she panted.

"Tell me how much."

"Fuck," she cried out, closing her legs and clutching the vibrating ball to her clit. "I'm coming, baby," she said, embracing the sensations that were exploding, sending shivers through every inch of her body. He was still until her breathing slowed as he toyed with the edge of the black lace. He ran his finger across the monarch butterfly tattooed in her right pelvic region, only fully visible when Payton was naked.

"Pretty," he said, removing her panty with a one-handed gesture, showing he was in control.

"Now, let me show you what my dick can do."

Chapter 7

Donathan awoke in the darkness, struggling to remember who he was and where he was. His mind was a jumble of thoughts and his head was throbbing as he attempted to stand up and get his bearings.

With no recollection of why he'd awakened naked, with his feet and one hand tied to the bed, he found himself standing there in this unfamiliar hotel room. Pieces of his clothing were scattered all over the floor. He grabbed his undershirt and pulled it over his head, then stuffed his arms into the sleeves of his dress shirt. What the hell was going on?

For the first time he noticed the clock on the nightstand. It read five a.m.

"Shit," he mumbled. He'd been out for hours.

He tried to remain calm, but the last thing he remembered was walking Austyn to her hotel room door. Was this her room? Had he entered?

There was no sign of her, but he took a look around and discovered an imprint of blood-red lipstick on an empty martini glass.

For a second he willed himself back to last night. Much to his regret, he'd arrived at Maxwell's alone. He and Sydney had argued briefly because she'd been called to the hospital to cover an overnight shift and she'd agreed to go even though she wasn't on call. His thoughts had moved on to Austyn. She'd shown up at Maxwell's, and after he autographed some headshots and took a few pictures, curiosity got the better of him and he'd joined her at the bar.

He rushed into the bathroom and splashed some cold water on his face, then soaped a fresh washcloth, washed himself off, and haphazardly buttoned his shirt. He hurried back into the room and stepped into his boxers, slacks, and jacket as quickly as he could.

Next, he patted down his pockets and found his keys and cell phone. He patted himself again, but this time he wasn't so lucky in locating the bulge he was looking for. No wallet. On impulse, he checked the nightstand.

"Fuck." Donathan grabbed his head to stop the echo. His temples were pulsating and his throat felt like sandpaper. He knelt to the floor, felt beneath the bed, but came up empty. He grabbed an unopened bottle of water off the small desk, turned it up to his mouth, and gulped half the liquid before bringing the plastic bottle down, fixated on it. It had to be the water. That was the only thing he remembered drinking.

Last night he'd talked with Austyn off and on for an hour. When she stood to leave, being the Good Samaritan he was, he'd offered to walk her to her car. That's when she'd informed him that she was new in town and was staying at the Courtyard Marriott, a few blocks over. He'd walked her to the hotel—to her room, but that was it—no more memory after that.

Donathan stuffed his black socks into his pocket and jammed his feet into his loafers. His normally sharp mind was dull, which caused his thoughts to be slow and heavy. It felt like he had a hangover, though he'd had only two in his lifetime. His last-minute jaunt to the men's room last night had left his opened bottle of water in Austyn's care, vulnerable to tampering. That fucking bitch must have drugged him.

Ten minutes later Donathan walked out of the building onto 9th and Broadway. He trolled the streets, looking for anything unusual, including the paparazzi. It was easy to brush off the made-up tabloid stories about him, but if a camera caught him stepping out of a hotel in a wrinkled Hugo Boss suit at this time of the morning, there would be no explaining away his actions to an eager freelance photographer.

He reached 13th Street, where he'd parked his car, and eased into the confines of his black Mercedes CL65 coupe, further assessing his situation. He could still hear Austyn's voice in his head. *You're the doctor who specializes in the art of sex.* Drugging him had been her plan from the start, he realized. She had arrived at the Richmond Country Club with every intention of luring him in.

He pulled away from the curb and didn't stop checking his rearview mirror until he merged onto I-80 east. The highway was empty; he coasted toward El Cerrito like a vampire trying to beat the rising of the sun.

All the way home, Donathan kept thinking about the nagging consequences of an unprotected sexual encounter. When he took the San Pablo exit, he was finally able to breathe, but he was aggravated. The images of glistening red lips and laughter mocked him. Did they even have sex? Of course they did. Right? Why else would he have been naked?

When Donathan pulled into his driveway, his headlights illuminated a small package propped against the mailbox. He exited the car to retrieve the parcel, and then he saw her. Across the street, his neighbor, Barbara Brown, sat perched in her front window, drinking her morning coffee, a ritual Donathan saw most Sunday mornings when he went out for his morning run. He looked down at his disheveled appearance. "Shit," he cursed softly.

Barbara Brown waved at him, and he knew exactly what that meant: She'd run and tell everyone who'd listen about his comings and goings, and eventually that would include Sydney. Now he had two problems. He stepped back into the car, held his head with one hand, and groaned at the throbbing as he reached the house at the end of the driveway. This would all look better once he got some rest, he told himself. He would take some Tylenol, get a few hours of sleep, then find that bitch Austyn and fix this.

Chapter 8

After she called Donathan and connected with his voice mail for what seemed like the hundredth time, Sydney left the hospital. Adrenaline surging, she wanted to squash their animosity once and for all.

In the past eight hours she'd called his cell phone at least a half-dozen times. He hadn't picked up, nor had he responded to her messages. Last night she'd chosen to cover an overnight shift instead of accompanying him to a promotional event, and she was sure eight hours hadn't done much for his disposition.

She understood why Donathan had been angry, but she didn't have the energy to rub elbows with hundreds of his aggressive fans. Her plans for last night had included pajamas, the couch, and *Pleasure* by Eric Jerome Dickey. Not flashbulbs and out-of-control women pawing at her husband.

Preoccupied with her thoughts, Sydney left the building, trudged toward her rental car, and nearly bumped into a security guard—a middle-aged man with crooked teeth, bifocal glasses, and salt-and-pepper hair dripping with Jheri curl juice. He was talking with Miles.

"I need a taxi," Miles said. "It's easier to use my spare key than to—"

"Taxi, where do you need to go?" Sydney questioned, stopping next to him.

Miles looked down at her, his dimple giving her a wink. "Home," he said, pasting a huge grin on his face. "I left my keys inside the car last night, and after ten minutes the alarm sets itself."

"Sounds like a pretty smart car," Sydney said as she peeked at her watch. She was on her way to the Oakland International Airport to pick up her cousin, Brea, whose plane wasn't due to land for another hour. That gave her plenty of time to do Miles a favor; after all, she owed him one.

"C'mon. I'll give you a ride."

"Oh . . . wow, thanks," Miles said appreciatively. "Let me grab the bag off the top of my car. I'll be right back."

Cars usually didn't impress Sydney, but the one with the small black duffel bag resting on top was sexy. It was black with tinted windows and had a high gloss that looked like it required hours of meticulous rubbing. The shiny machine looked like something from a *Back to the Future* or *Batman Returns* movie.

Sydney stared at Miles as he maneuvered through the parking lot. He had a certain style that stirred up the laws of attraction, but as he slid into the passenger seat next to her she wondered what his shiny, attention-grabbing toy was compensating for. She hoped it was nothing catastrophic because as far as she was concerned he was perfect—for Payton.

"Where to?"

"Jack London Square. The Ellington on Broadway."

On the way to Miles's condominium, Sydney drove down Telegraph, their conversation simple and easy. He had only been on the neurosurgery team for a couple of months, but they talked nonstop, as if they'd known each other for years. This made her plan to uncover whatever he was compensating for and whether he was right for Payton. At first she'd toyed with the idea that because he was a good-looking man, he was probably full of himself. Most men got off on talking about themselves. But then again, so did Payton.

"Why are you smiling?" he suddenly asked.

"Um . . . I didn't realize I was."

"Yeah, you were *cheesing* real hard," he teased.

"I was?"

"Yes, you were."

"I was thinking about my cousin," she answered vaguely.

"And why would thinking of your cousin make you smile?"

"Well, she's flying into town today. She's been overseas for work, so I haven't seen her in a while. Family always makes me smile."

"I know what you mean. I'm big on family, too. Just wish California wasn't so far away from mine and the south side of Chicago."

"Sounds like you're having trouble adjusting to the move."

Miles nodded. His eyes were dark and intense. "I guess you could say that." He chuckled. "All I've seen since I moved here is the Uptown District of downtown Oakland and Jack London Square, which shouldn't count because I live there. Mostly, I miss my daughters."

Bingo. It all made sense. His nonchalant attitude when she'd mentioned Payton. She'd been so busy trying to hook him up, she'd missed the obvious. Miles was married. Deflated, she stole a quick glance at his ring finger. There was no ring, but that didn't mean he wasn't married.

"So, when are your wife and girls moving here? It must be hard being separated from them."

"Being separated from my girls is one of the hardest things I've ever had to do, but unfortunately, they won't be moving to California. I'm divorced and they live with their mother in Chicago. They're excited about coming to visit, though. They think Mickey Mouse and I are next-door neighbors," he said, motioning for her to turn onto 3rd Street and stop in front of a modern concrete building.

"I'll be right back."

Miles jumped out of the car, hurried toward the double doors, and disappeared into the building. Sydney smiled again. Miles was perfect. He wasn't an asshole and he wasn't married, which was the total opposite of the losers Payton seemed to attract. His children added a small complication, but that barrier was greatly diminished because they lived in another state. Now all Sydney had to do was get Payton and Miles in the same room and the rest would take care of itself. She fished her cell phone out of her bag and checked it one more time to make sure Donathan hadn't called her—a wasted effort—then she texted Payton: **Are you still coming to Napa today? Call me when you get this.**

Several minutes later Miles was back in the car.

"Thanks," he said, holding up a key, a little out of breath from his jaunt.

"No problem."

As Sydney made a U-turn and headed back in the direction of Children's Hospital, she became more determined that Miles was going to meet Payton today. "So when are you leaving for the conference?" she asked.

"I'm flying in tomorrow to spend some time with my family and to catch the Bulls game on Wednesday—"

"The Chicago Bulls," Sydney squealed. "Me too. My husband thinks I'm crazy for going solo, but there's no way I can go to Chicago and not see the house that Jordan built. I can't wait."

Miles looked up. "Well, I agree with your husband. The United Center isn't in the safest part of town. I have extra seats in the box. I could pick you up," he said gently.

Sydney bounced his idea around for a second, then answered yes with a sheepish grin planted on her face. This was the perfect segue for her unsolicited invitation.

"Miles, a group of us are going up to Napa for a wine-tasting event this afternoon. How would you like to join us?"

Chapter 9

The pristine white Charger Limousine pulled into Copia's circular driveway, coming to a stop in the passenger loading zone. Sydney checked on Donathan one last time while Brea and Miles continued to chat about her life as a music executive.

Things weren't going as Sydney had planned today. First, when she'd gotten home this morning, she and Brea had found Donathan wrapped in the guest-room covers, a distressed look on his face, saying he'd caught a twenty-four-hour bug and wouldn't be accompanying them to Napa. Then Payton had responded to her previously sent text with a vague: **Yes, but a change of plans...I'll meet you there**. Sydney hadn't heard from her since, and if Payton didn't show, her setup for today would be pointless.

The driver opened the door and Brea stepped out of the limo dressed to kill in a Valentino white linen suit. She consulted her watch, then opened her Swarovski crystal–decorated clutch purse, the jewels catching the afternoon sunlight. It was early April and the California heat was unseasonable.

"Cousin," she said to Sydney, "finish your wine. I have to go to the dressing room to check on my artist. Here are three tickets. I'll catch up with you all later."

Sydney watched from the tinted limousine window as Brea hurried toward the building and the stares of people littering the walkway, hoping to see somebody famous.

Ten minutes later, with still no word from Payton, Sydney led the way, edging along the cobblestoned building. Once inside, she stopped at the will-call window to leave Payton's ticket. As soon as Sydney finished the transaction, her cell phone rang.

"Excuse me, I need to take this," Sydney said to Miles. She stepped out of earshot and answered.

"It's about freaking time. Where the hell are you?" Sydney said into the phone.

"Well, I missed you, too, pumpkin." Payton giggled.

"What happened? I thought you were driving up with us in the limo."

"Nothing happened. I was in the middle of something and decided to drive up on my own. Is that a crime?"

"No, it's not a crime, but may I remind you that it was your brilliant idea that we all ride up together so we wouldn't have to assign anyone as the designated driver."

Sydney looked up and found Miles staring at her: a long, penetrating stare. She felt herself getting warm.

"I know, but like I said, something came up. Is everything all right?"

"Everything is fine."

"You seem a little agitated, like you need a drink."

"Well," Sydney said, continuing to observe Miles, her mind racing in a thousand directions. She watched as women took notice, drawn to his confident edge. "We'd planned on waiting until you arrived to start tasting. How long before you get here?"

"I'll be at least another twenty minutes. So I think you and Donathan better start without me."

For a second Sydney contemplated telling Payton that Donathan was home sick and Miles was a part of the *we* she'd been referring to, but she weighed her thoughts and quickly came to her senses. Miles was definitely a viable prospect for Payton, and if Sydney wanted this to work, she had to make sure the timing was right.

"All right. We'll see you in a few."

A jazz quintet serenaded people perched at the linen-covered tables and scattered on blankets across the amphitheater lawn.

Miles placed his hand at the small of Sydney's back and ushered her toward the African American Vintners, who took cover underneath canvas tasting tents stationed at the end of the winding patio. She was feeling quite comfortable with this man. As they reached the pavilion, Miles leaned forward, his warm breath kissing her ear.

"Are you a red or a white drinker?"

Sydney swallowed hard. "Um, I'm a white girl."

"Have you ever tried a Viognier?"

"Vio who?" she responded, caught off guard by the surge of energy moving through her body. Miles leaned in close again.

"It's pronounced VEE-ohn-yay."

Sydney shook her head. "No. I've never heard of it."

"It's made from a very rare white grape originally grown almost exclusively in the Northern Rhône region of France, but its popularity in the States is increasing. The aroma smells like apricots and tangerines."

"Sounds tasty. It's not too sweet, is it?"

"What do you usually drink?"

"Riesling."

"Then I think you're going to find it very pleasing to your palate."

Three glasses of Viognier and an hour later, Sydney was in love and heavily buzzed. She left Miles in search of bottled water—tipsy was okay, but drunk wasn't an option. After finding a bottle of water, she wandered around Copia, mingling her way through the crowd, and ended up next to a pair of unfamiliar faces. She hadn't seen Brea since they'd arrived, and Payton hadn't made her grand entrance—yet.

Sydney gulped down the water while replaying the last hour in her mind. She'd always had an overactive imagination, one that sometimes got her into trouble, but she wasn't imagining this: his long, penetrating stares—the heavy breathing in her ear—and he kept touching her. It might have been subtle, but Dr. Miles Day was flirting with her.

"Ladies and gentlemen, please put your hands together for

Warner recording artist Jabari," the announcer, with a high-glossed shine bouncing off his bald head, crooned into the microphone.

Out of the corners of her eyes, Sydney noticed the multi-platinum R&B singer stroll onto the stage, clad in a wifebeater, jean shorts, Timberland boots, and fresh cornrows.

"What the hell is he wearing?" she mumbled in total disbelief.

With her target in sight, Payton eased her way through the crowd murmuring, "Excuse me" and "Pardon me," trying her best not to step on anyone's toes as she passed.

Brea was glowing as she extracted herself from conversation with a pencil-thin woman in full African dress and stepped forward to greet her. Ever since they'd met in college, Payton remembered Brea working hard to achieve perfection, and from the looks of things she'd gotten pretty damn close. Brea's medium-brown eyes glimmered, the color of molten amber. She'd never seen her look prettier.

"Oh my God! Girl, look at you," Payton said, embracing Brea tightly, but Payton frowned once her attention shifted to the stage. "What's up with that outfit y'all got on him? I know he's into the ghetto-thug look, but what about dressing him for the crowd? He looks like a hot mess."

"You're preaching to the choir," Brea said, sounding slightly annoyed. "He was supposed to wear a simple white linen two-piece, but I've been fighting with him for the last forty-five minutes and couldn't get him to put it on. Now his ass is up there not only embarrassing himself but he's a direct reflection on me. I'm so tired of these damn artists."

The sound of Jabari's soothing and sexy voice pulled their attention back to the stage.

"Well, at least he sounds good; let's hope people just close their eyes and sway to the music without looking at him."

Brea shook her head and chuckled. "Girl, you are c-r-a-z-y."

"So where's Sydney?" Payton asked, looking around the enclosed courtyard.

"I'm not sure. She and Miles are probably—"

"Miles? Where's Donathan?"

"He's at home sick. Miles is—"

"A doctor who works with her," they said in unison.

"Sydney has made it a point to tell me all about Dr. Miles," Payton said, shaking her head and rolling her eyes upward.

"Well, you might want to start listening because the brotha isn't bad on the eyes."

"Whatever," Payton responded. "I'm not letting your cousin play matchmaker for me anymore." She scanned the crowd a second time and caught sight of Sydney standing next to a tall, dark, and very handsome man in his early forties. Even with all the striking people in the venue, Miles stood out.

He was dressed in a pair of cream-colored slacks and a salmon tailored shirt that gently clung to his chest and washboard abs. A smile played around the corners of Payton's glossed lips as she gave him another once-over for good measure. She lingered at the bulge between his legs. Miles was a man with confidence and he looked like he had a nice package. Her kind of guy. She briefly watched him being overly attentive—the perfect gentleman, but what she wanted to know was if he could get buck wild in the bedroom. Feeling a sudden rush of lust, she excused herself.

"I'll be right back."

Payton grabbed a glass of wine from a passing waiter and sipped the amber liquid as she made her way over, careful not to damage the heels of her four-inch Louboutin's between the cracks of the patio. Without warning, a woman scooted her chair into Payton's path, causing her to slip, lose her balance, and stumble into Miles, a river of wine flowing freely down the front of his shirt and her silk blouse.

"Shit," Payton mumbled, disengaging herself from Miles, whose hands were warm as they rested at the small of her back.

The obese woman grabbed a handful of napkins and was up blotting at the wet spots that had soaked through the fabrics.

"Oh my God! I'm sorry. I am so sorry," the woman said, apologizing profusely.

"It's fine. At least the wine was white," Payton assured her with a half smile, but truth be told, she wished the bitch would sit back down.

She looked up at Miles. "I'm really sorry for stumbling into you like that," she said, eyeing the woman.

"Do I get an apology, too?" Sydney questioned, her hands now perched on both hips. Payton threw her a sideways glance and smiled. Sydney was wearing a peach crochet wrap dress that hugged her small waist and accentuated her breasts nicely. Her friend looked beautiful, confident—and tipsy. Payton playfully ignored her, extending her hand to Miles.

"I'm Payton Jones," she said, licking her lips seductively.

"Ah . . . Payton," he said, flashing his dimpled smile. "Sydney has told me all about you."

Payton smiled knowingly.

"Well, I hope she left some things to your imagination."

Chapter 10

Sydney stood in the guest bedroom doorway, watching her husband sleep. She'd been up a few hours, had had breakfast with Brea, and had just put her into the car service that was taking her back to the Oakland airport.

A perplexing thought came to Sydney. Was Donathan really sick or was his twenty-four-hour bug simply retaliation against her for not going to Maxwell's with him on Saturday?

Last night Sydney had arrived home from Napa, tipsy and sexually charged. Once Brea dozed off, Sydney had showered, put on some nice lingerie, and then tiptoed into the guest room, where Donathan had retreated. His eyes were closed, but a pair of white earbuds, connected to his iPod, dangled from his ears. She crawled into bed, straddled him, and gently tugged at the white cord, popping the earphones from his ears. She leaned down and kissed him.

"Baby," she whispered seductively, "I'm sorry about Saturday night. I really should have gone to Maxwell's with you."

For a while Donathan didn't say a word; he just lay there before he mechanically opened his eyes, stared at the ceiling, and simply said, "Yes, you should have."

Sydney could tell by the terseness of his words that he still wasn't too happy with her.

"Look, Donathan, I said I'm sorry. What else do you want me to do?"

"Nothing," he said before he replaced the earbuds and closed his eyes like she wasn't there.

She was speechless. He never reacted like that. If it were up to Donathan, they would have sex every night, and not the quickie variety. She loved sex, too, but if they missed a night or two, it wasn't the end of the world. She could never remember a time when Donathan hadn't succumbed to her advances. So retaliation definitely explained the anticlimactic ending to last night.

Sydney moved toward him and shook him gently. "Donathan. Donathan—"

"What?" he tossed back, rolling over to face her. She could feel the click as they locked eyes briefly, and then he reached for the layers of bedsheets wafted around her feet. He jerked the covers up around his neck and turned his back to her.

"Honey, you need to get up. You're going to be late for work."

"I'm not going into the office today," he mumbled. "I canceled my patients."

This was getting more bizarre by the minute. In all their years of marriage, she only remembered him canceling patients one other time, and that was when he'd contracted chicken pox while doing volunteer work at the local homeless shelter. But whatever was going on with him now was clearly not as visible as those little red dots had been.

She sat on the edge of the bed and leaned over to inspect him further, hoping to catch a glimpse of what was ailing him. She slid into bed beside him and gently raked her fingers over his closely cropped hair, her breasts pressing against his back.

"Sweetie," she murmured, "what's wrong?"

"Damn! What is it you don't understand about *I don't feel well*?" he asked, his voice rising.

Sydney jumped up as if she'd been tased and placed both hands on her hips. She was getting more aggravated by the minute. At first she'd been swimming in worry about Donathan, but this odd, hostile behavior was beginning to get on her nerves.

"Okay, I give up," she said, tossing her hands into the air. "You might be a little under the weather, but that's no reason for you to talk to me so rudely."

She was halfway out the door when the security intercom sounded. She waited for him to move, but he didn't.

Rolling her eyes in exasperation, Sydney said, "Don't you want to get that?"

"What sense does that make, Sydney? You're already up—"

"Well, you're fully clothed, and in case you hadn't noticed, I'm not dressed yet."

After Donathan let the housekeeper in, he finally managed to leave the guest room where he'd held himself captive for more than twenty-four hours. His plan was to make a few calls, check his email, and cancel his credit cards. He slipped into his home office and turned on the flat-screen television to fill the empty space with noise. He sat down and leaned back in his desk chair. On a day like today he and Sydney should be lying in bed naked, savoring the afterglow of good sex. Instead, he was treating her like shit. Last night's memory of Sydney in that sexy lingerie tugged at him while he listened to Dave Clark, of *Mornings on 2*, recite the morning news.

"Well, good morning to you, welcome back. The time is now eight-thirty. We have new information this morning about the victim of a brutal attack in Richmond late last week. The unidentified man found in a hotel room bleeding from life-threatening injuries has died. The police are looking for an attractive twenty-something female who was seen entering the hotel room with the victim and are asking for the public's help in catching the person responsible for these crimes."

Donathan turned down the volume, his frown deepening. Sydney had made her way to the guest room apologetic, tipsy, and horny, the perfect recipe for mind-blowing sex, but he'd purposely shut her down. That was the first time he'd done that, and if he did it twice, there would be no type of sickness that could explain it away, which was why he had been so abrupt with her a few minutes earlier. All he had to do was keep her pissed off for one more day and then she'd leave for the medical conference in Chicago, giving him the breathing room he needed to concentrate and sort out his situation.

Donathan thought back to when he'd first met Austyn at the country club. Even though he'd noted something odd about her, something he just couldn't put his finger on, he'd determined she was a little off-balance. And when she showed up at Maxwell's, although his first reaction had been concern, that had quickly dissipated when he weighed the fact that the event had been publicized on the radio for weeks. Anyone who listened to his show knew exactly where he would be on Saturday night. His stomach growled, reminding him that he hadn't eaten since yesterday, so he made a detour to the kitchen.

After he'd downed some eggs, turkey sausage, and biscuits, Donathan headed back to his office. He picked up the small box he'd left on the foyer table yesterday morning and a new envelope with the same label—*urgent*—propped beside it. The packages were addressed to him but were devoid of a return address. He set them both on his desk, reached for a letter opener, and creased the top flap of the box. Inside, a small lavender envelope was perched on top of packing peanuts that hid the contents of the box. Donathan ripped open the small envelope, his eyes quickly scanning the words on the paper.

Doc,
You were much better in bed than I had anticipated, although I think I taught you a thing or two☺. Let's get together soon to create some new experiences. Oh, and I don't need this anymore, but I thought you might. Until next time . . .
—A

He dumped the contents of the box onto his desk and found his wallet. He opened it, fanning the contents as if his life depended on it. Everything except his cash was present and accounted for.

"That crazy bitch," he hissed through gritted teeth. He grabbed the letter opener again and slit the flap of the envelope.

"Donathan," Sydney called out to him.

Her voice startled him and the envelope slipped from his grasp, spilling the contents onto the floor. His heart stopped, then flipflopped inside his chest as he stared at pictures of himself naked, with a naked Austyn straddling him.

"Honey," Sydney called again, "I'm going to the grocery store and to run a few errands." Donathan could hear the sound of her footfalls coming toward his office door. He jumped up, stepped into the foyer, and closed the door tightly behind him.

"Can you write a check for Esther? Are you all right?" Sydney asked, brushing her hand down the side of his face. He jerked away as if her hand was hot. She narrowed her eyes, scanned him, trying to make sense of his bizarre behavior.

"You need to go to the doctor to get checked out?"

"No. I'm fine. I just ate something a few minutes ago and now I feel like I want to throw up. I'm sure whatever I have is viral and will pass in a few days."

Sydney felt his head again to see if he had a fever. This time he had sense enough not to move.

"You are a little warm, but that's probably because of all those clothes you have on. Do you have a headache?" she asked.

He kissed her on the cheek, hoping to cut her interrogation short, and nudged her toward the front door.

"I'll be fine."

"Did you get the package Esther brought inside for you? She mentioned she'd placed a letter-sized envelope on the table."

His body tensed at the mention of the envelope. "Yes, I got it. I was about to open it—"

"Do you need me to bring you anything back from the store?"

Donathan had an answer ready. "Bring me some chicken noodle soup and some Gatorade."

He needed Sydney to leave so he could be alone with his thoughts.

"Okay. Don't forget to write the check for Esther, and give her an extra fifty."

"I'll take care of it right now," he said. Hell, he'd give Esther an extra hundred if that was what it took to get Sydney out of the house.

"I'll be back in a few hours."

No sooner had the front door closed than Donathan was back in his office. He scooped the pictures up off the floor and studied them. He couldn't believe this bullshit. He scrutinized the note from the box again, then picked up his wallet and located Austyn's business card. On his iPhone he pressed ★67 to shield his number, then dialed. It rang several times before her voice mail picked up. He knew better than to leave his name in the message; any man who didn't should have paid attention to the Tiger Woods fiasco. He waited for the beep and then spoke.

"You know who this is; we need to talk." He hesitated for a moment, as if he wanted to say something further but thought better of it and ended the call.

Donathan leaned back in his chair, totally frustrated. If Sydney ever saw those pictures, it would be the end of his marriage as he knew it, and there was no way he was losing his wife over that stupid shit. He had no idea what Austyn wanted from him, but the pictures screamed blackmail. A lot of people would pay a lot of money to get their hands on those pictures. He was a local celebrity and unfortunately, anything he did was news. He needed to work fast. He needed to find out how much money Austyn wanted to make this nightmare go away.

Chapter 11

Standing outside the red-brick building, Joi White was confused as she clutched her two boys by the hand. She was dressed in a velour sweat suit like she was on her way to the gym, in contrast to the professionally dressed people who entered the double glass doors. They were on their way to work, she presumed. Once she caught a glimpse of her reflection, she tried in vain to relax the distressed look on her face that disrupted her soft, feminine features.

On Saturday Tyrese had found the tape recorder she'd planted underneath their bed. He'd been on his best behavior for the rest of the weekend, but she wasn't stupid; she knew his ass was up to something. The fact was, Tyrese was cheating on her and she'd finally gotten up the nerve to do something about it.

Without further ado, Joi took a deep breath and walked into the reception area of the law office. She assisted her four-year-old twin boys into empty seats and handed them two small Ziploc bags filled with action figures from her tote. When she'd called for this appointment last week, the only time they'd had available was before she could drop the kids off at preschool, so she had no choice but to bring them along with her.

"Mommy needs you to sit right here, play with your toys, and be really quiet," she said, kissing them both on the forehead. "If you're good, we'll go for ice cream when I pick you up from school today. Okay?"

Both boys nodded vigorously in unison.

When she looked up, she saw an older woman sitting behind the desk—a voluptuous, bleached blonde with horribly applied eyelashes. The woman sneered at the sight of the boys, even though they hadn't done one thing to warrant her scorn.

Skipping the pleasantries, Joi started in. "I'm here to see Mr. Morgan."

"Do you have an appointment, ma'am?"

Joi's face grew warm with irritation. Now the woman was insinuating that Joi had just sauntered in off the street without an appointment?

"Of course I have an appointment," Joi snapped, giving the receptionist a hard stare. The woman cleared her throat.

"Your name, ma'am?"

"Mrs. Joi White," she said, emphasizing the Mrs.

The receptionist gathered a small stack of papers, attached them to a clipboard, and handed them to her. "Fill out these papers and I'll let Mr. Morgan know you're here."

Joi snatched the clipboard and sat down next to the boys, her lips pursed in a tight grimace. That bitch had a lot of nerve giving her a hard time. She began filling in the blanks on the form and stopped at the last question, which asked the reason for her visit today. She didn't really want a divorce, but Tyrese was giving her no choice. They'd been married for eight years. Before they'd said *I do* she'd put up with the womanizing, but once they were married, she'd expected his behavior to change. But it hadn't.

"Mrs. White," the receptionist called out to her, avoiding eye contact, "Mr. Morgan will see you now."

Joi looked over at her children, playing quietly with their toys. Divorce was a big step that would change their lives. They didn't deserve this.

"Now let's pinky swear on our deal." Both boys eagerly raised a pinky into the air and Joi hooked her pinkies in theirs. "Mommy won't take long, I promise," she said, then headed toward the open door with *Chase Morgan* etched on the nameplate.

"Excuse me, ma'am. Ma'am," the receptionist called after her. "You can't leave these children out here unattended."

Ignoring the woman's demand, Joi entered Mr. Morgan's office, handed him the clipboard, and sat down in the chair facing his massive cherrywood desk. He was a round man, shaped like a plump California raisin, with a full head of salt-and-pepper hair.

"What can I do for you today, um, Mrs. White?" he asked, referencing the stack of papers in front of him.

"I'd like some information about filing for a divorce," Joi responded, hoping she'd come to the right place to get the answers she needed.

The portly man leaned back in his massive leather chair and chuckled. "Well, you've come to the right place for that. What seems to be the problem, if you don't mind me asking?"

"I think my husband is cheating on me. Can you help me find out if he is?"

"Listen, Mrs. White," Chase Morgan said, "I'm a divorce attorney, but I don't help to determine if husbands—or wives, for that matter—are cheating. Normally, my clients come to see me once that's been determined, and then I help with the divorce."

"Well, then, I need to know if he's cheating before you can help me," she said, smiling sweetly at him—hypnotized by the steam from his coffee cup as it dissipated into the air.

"Well, I don't think you've determined if you want a divorce or not. So my advice right now is for you to prepare in case you decide to go ahead with a divorce," he said, picking up a pen with his free hand. "Now, what does your husband do for a living?"

She reluctantly responded, "He works for the Golden State Warriors."

"Is he a player?"

"Not anymore," she said with a slight hesitation. "A knee injury ended his career a few years ago. Now he's in management."

Chase Morgan sat up straight and rested his pen on the blank pad in front of him. Joi could see the dollar signs dancing in his pupils.

"Is your husband Tyrese White?"

"Yes." She sighed heavily, as if a huge weight had been lifted.

"Does your husband know you're here?"

"No."

The fat man leaned across his desk, closing the distance between them. He cleared his throat and whispered like he was telling her a secret. "Listen, Mrs. White, this is what you need to do. Gather data quietly. Get bank statements, bills, real estate documents. Anything that shows assets you might be entitled to. If your husband finds out you came to see me today, he'll probably start hiding assets, like most men do—"

"How do I find out if he's cheating?"

They were interrupted by a light knock on the door, followed by a muffled female voice.

"Mr. Morgan, your next appointment is here."

Joi watched in annoyance as he rose to his feet. There was no way her fifteen-minute consultation was over. He reached into a desk drawer and took out a business card.

"Mrs. White, let's be real. If you suspect your husband is cheating, you and I both know the odds are that he is. But if you need concrete proof, hire a private investigator," he said, giving her the business card.

A private investigator? Of course. Why hadn't she thought of that?

"Call that number. I'm sure Holsey will be able to help you."

"Thank you," she said, smiling awkwardly and shaking his free hand.

"Now, once you get the proof you need, make sure you come back here and let me help you with your divorce." He grinned. "But between now and then, remember your husband doesn't know you came to see me today and I suggest you keep it that way."

When she'd reentered the reception area, the receptionist sat in horror as a sea of decapitated action figures littered the floor. She'd scolded the boys more times than she could remember about taking better care of their toys. Those figures cost money.

"What's going on?"

"Don't worry, Mommy," Terrance, the older twin said. "We were just playing a game. We can fix them again. Look."

Joi looked on as the twins struggled vainly to reattach a head to a body. Sweat began to bead on their foreheads. She glanced back at the receptionist and smiled.

The younger twin said, "I can do it, Mommy. I've done it before."

"That's not the point, Taylor. You shouldn't have pulled their heads off in the first place."

"It's not my fault; they were trying to kill Thor," he said.

His expression was so adorably earnest; it was a struggle for her not to laugh.

With a newfound direction, Joi was relieved as she left the law office. She fastened the boys in their booster seats and couldn't wait a moment longer to use her cell phone to dial the number listed on the business card. She stood outside the SUV.

"Curtis Holsey," a voice said in a smoker's baritone.

"Uh, Mr. Holsey, I was referred to you by my attorney, Chase Morgan. I'd like to hire you for some personal business—"

"I charge a five-thousand-dollar retainer and I don't give refunds—"

"Five thousand dollars? What do I get for that kind of money?"

"Peace of mind and answers to your questions," he said, his voice scratchy and hoarse. "Before I begin work on your case, I need the retainer in cash, a picture of who you want investigated, his vehicle license plate number, and the address where he works. Can you meet me this afternoon?"

"Hold on a second, let me check my calendar." Joi paused, thoughts flashing through her head. There was no way she could access that kind of cash without Tyrese questioning her about it. She could borrow it from her brother, but that would take a few days. Suddenly, an idea popped into her head. She would take the money out of their savings account, and when Tyrese asked, she'd say her mother couldn't pay her property taxes and needed a loan.

"Call me back when you're serious," he croaked into the phone.

"No, wait! Can you meet me in Concord in an hour?" she asked, still hoping to make her eleven o'clock Aspire Pilates class.

"Meet me at the Willows Shopping Center, in the front lot closest to Claim Jumper. I'll be in a dark blue Toyota Corolla."

A little over an hour had passed when Joi turned her Mercedes G Wagon into the Willows Shopping Center parking lot. She'd dropped the boys at preschool, stopped at the bank to withdraw the cash, and made a quick stop at home to grab the items Holsey had requested. She immediately spotted the navy-blue Toyota Corolla, parked a few spaces away, and approached with caution. When she reached the driver's side window, a pair of pale-blue eyes looked up, eyeballing her all over. He was holding a camera and beckoned her toward the passenger seat.

"Get in," he barked.

Clutching her tote bag, Joi reluctantly moved around the car. This wasn't at all what she'd expected. Curtis Holsey had dishwater-brown hair and leathery, worn skin, and his shoulders were hunched forward, making his back look like he was hiding something under his shirt. When she opened the passenger door the seat was littered with empty coffee cups before Holsey swept them to the floor. A stained cloth seat stared back at her. Her apprehensions grew. Who knew what dangers awaited her in this man's car? What if he was a murderer? Then she remembered he'd been referred to her by an attorney and she relaxed. If this man could help her get actual proof that Tyrese was cheating, this was worth it. She eased into the seat but left the door slightly ajar.

"I'm Joi White. I think my husband is cheating on me," she said, coughing from the overpowering smell of second-hand cigarette smoke.

"Well, who else would you be? Did you bring the stuff I requested?" He raised the camera and aimed it at the Hilton Hotel across the street. His stubby right index finger pressed the button and snapped a picture.

Without letting the tote bag out of her grasp, Joi reached inside and pulled out a manila envelope. "Everything is right here. The pictures of Tyrese, his license plate number, where he works. All the items you asked me to bring. Are you going to follow him and take pictures?"

"The money?" Holsey questioned, never moving his gaze away from the camera lens or bothering to answer her last question.

"Yeah, I have that, too," she said, fishing out the size-ten envelope that contained fifty crisp $100 bills. She extended the money in his direction.

"Place the envelope in my glove compartment," he said before he snapped another picture.

Joi opened the glove box and stared at several other size-ten envelopes, all matching hers in size. She reluctantly placed hers on top, then gently closed the glove box, careful not to disturb the ashtray full of cigarettes and ashes. She stared at the disheveled man, her curiosity getting the better of her.

"Are you really a private detective?" Joi asked, actually sounding vaguely interested.

Holsey looked away from the camera and made eye contact with her for the first time. His beady eyes, now ice-blue, unnerved her. He nodded. "Pays the bills and besides, I'm only spying on the bad guys... and girls," he said, focusing his attention back toward the hotel.

Joi anxiously looked down at her watch. "I have to go," she said, fully opening the car door. She hesitated before she placed her feet on the asphalt and then turned to look at him. "Will you call me?"

"Is the number you called me from earlier a good one to reach you?" he responded, still focused on his task at hand.

Joi nodded.

"Well, if your husband is doing anything—and I mean anything at all—I'll get you what you need to nail the son of a bitch."

Joi exited the Corolla, pleased by his last response. She prayed that beneath the cigarette-hazed exterior, the man who looked like he was the one who should be followed was sincere in his promise and closed the car door behind her.

Chapter 12

By the time Sydney made it to the front of the security line at the Oakland International Airport, she was willing herself not to panic. In thirty minutes her flight was scheduled to depart from gate twenty-nine, and if she missed it, she wouldn't make the Chicago Bulls basketball game. She handed the TSA agent her boarding pass and identification, then waited impatiently while he performed the verification. The car service had picked her up a half hour earlier than recommended; otherwise, curb service or not, there'd be no way she'd make this flight to Chicago.

After passing through the metal detector and reclaiming her belongings, Sydney hurried toward the departure gate like she was running the Nike Women's Marathon. When she arrived at the gate, she was confused by the lack of passengers boarding but relaxed when the gate agent told her the flight had been delayed about twenty minutes. She slipped into the ladies' room to freshen up. When she returned to the gate, she pulled out her cell phone and dialed Donathan's number.

He'd come home late last night, after she'd gone to bed, and had left this morning at the crack of dawn. It was ridiculous that she lived in the same house with Donathan but, over the last few days, the only way she could actually have a conversation with him was to call him on his cell phone. She walked over to the window, gazed out at the sea of airplanes parked at the gates, and listened as the phone rang and rang. She checked her watch. This was the time he usually left the radio station for his office, but he left a note saying he was having breakfast with his mother before work. Her call went immediately to voice mail and she was about to leave him a very nasty message but thought better of it and ended the call. At that very moment she decided there was no reason for her to wallow in negative thoughts because of Donathan's unusual behavior. He was acting strange, but maybe he really was just under the weather. Whatever it was, she refused to let it keep her in a foul mood. The truth was she was on her way to Chicago and her plan was to have a good time.

As soon as Sydney boarded the airplane, she noticed a white woman with piercing blue eyes and strawberry-blond hair waving to her. Shit, Sydney thought, taking a deep breath as she staggered toward the waving woman. It was Julia Stevens, a colleague of hers. The last thing she wanted to do was sit next to chatty Julia on a four-hour flight to Chicago. She was seated near the window, looking as if she'd just stepped out of the pages of *InStyle* magazine. She wore a crisp white button-down, starched khakis, and patent leather loafers.

"Sydney, darling, I saw you step into the ladies' room, so I took the liberty of reserving you a seat. I hope you don't mind," Julia said. She placed an elongated white capsule in her mouth and chased it with bottled water. She returned the cap back to the water bottle and fished around in her carry-on bag, which rested on the middle seat.

"That was an antihistamine," Julia said, neatly tying a silk scarf around a travel pillow. "Whenever I fly, I get these terrible sinus pressure headaches. The good news is the antihistamine works wonders. The bad news is it puts me into an immediate sleep coma."

"Well, I'm sure you'd prefer sleep over a headache," Sydney said, excited to learn this little arrangement might not be so bad after all. She took the aisle seat, removed her book, and slid her bag beneath the seat in front of her.

"Absolutely." Julia yawned. "I was up half the night packing, which I used to do purposely so I'd be able to sleep on the plane. But now with the pill I don't have to worry about sleep. I guess old habits die hard," Julia said, sliding her carry-on under the seat in front of her. She fluffed the silk-covered pillow, pulled a satin mask over her eyes, and shifted her body to rest against the covered airplane window. "Wake me when we land in the Windy City," she said, and then pulled a cashmere blanket up over her shoulders.

After buckling herself in, Sydney stared at the cover of the erotic novel she'd started reading a few days before. She'd found herself craving the story like the sexual addiction of the woman she was reading about. In fact, the things they did in *Pleasure* aroused her so much she'd masturbated three times over the course of the past few days. Sydney realized it was only partly because of the hot-and-sensual content on almost every page; it was also the lack of sexual activity between her and Donathan. They hadn't had sex in almost a week, which was highly unusual.

Sick or not, she felt there was something going on. She shook her head and fought off the feeling of dread threatening to alter her mood again. Not more than fifteen minutes ago she'd vowed to let this go, and here it was creeping up again. She pressed her back into the seat, opened the book, and vowed once again to deal with Donathan and his nonsense when she returned.

Donathan sat behind his glass-topped desk, trying to mask his distress. It had been two days since he'd left the first message on Austyn's voice mail and, to his chagrin, many more had followed. He still hadn't heard from her. He sifted through the patient files, stopping at the name that matched the one listed next on his schedule, and scooped the others back into a disheveled pile. He'd only seen one patient this morning, but he hadn't been able to concentrate. A light rap at the slightly ajar door was followed by his receptionist, Elaine, poking her head in. He looked at her, then back to the file in front of him.

"Yes?"

"Dr. James, there's a woman out here named Austyn Greene to see you. She doesn't have an appointment but insists you'll see her. I told the young woman we were very busy today and I'd be happy to make her an appointment for tomorrow, but she won't take no for an answer—"

Donathan nodded, his nerves momentarily soothed by this development. Finally he could put this madness to rest. He wanted to jump up and give Elaine a high-five. His little problem had found her way to him. It didn't get any better than that. He stood and adjusted his gabardine slacks.

"I'll see Ms. Greene now. Send her in."

A few seconds later Donathan greeted Austyn at the door. He grabbed her by the arm and yanked her into his office, closing the door behind her.

"What the fuck do you think you're doing?" he said, his voice angry and low.

Austyn tossed her head back and laughed. "Well, I thought you'd be happy to see me and I guess I was right because this rough shit is turning me the fuck on," she purred and held his eyes. "If you want me to, I can just go away and—"

Donathan couldn't believe she had the audacity to glide into his office like nothing had happened. But he needed to get a hold of himself. "Have a seat," he said before he released her arm and watched her turn on her leopard-print platforms and saunter toward the leather sofa. His eyes lingered on the skin-tight pencil skirt palming her ass and cursed at himself for noticing. Austyn seated herself, crossed her legs, and stared up at him. After a few minutes of intense stares, he took a seat opposite her in his wing-back chair.

"Am I making you nervous?" she flirted.

Hell yeah, he was nervous, Donathan thought, but he didn't say it out loud. With Austyn he believed he would learn a lot more from listening than he would from talking.

She gave him a daring look. "Well, they say sex is the best way to ruin a friendship. I hope it didn't mess up ours."

Donathan cleared his throat and responded in an even tone. "So we had sex?"

"Of course we did, silly." She giggled and paused for a beat. "What? You don't remember?"

"Unfortunately, thanks to you, I don't. What did you use to drug me?"

Austyn stiffened. "*Drug* is such a harsh word. I just helped you relax a little. I thought your memory might be a problem, which is the reason I sent you the pictures. I know you couldn't see your face in those shots, but I have *others*—"

Others? What the hell did she mean? Donathan tried to get a read on her so he could decide what angle to take, but it was hard because he didn't know her well enough. He knew better than to believe the only reason for the pictures was to make sure he remembered. And he was also clear that, no matter what she said, she definitely had a *reason* for the *other* pictures. He just needed to find out what that reason was.

"What can I do for you, Austyn?" he said, leaning back in the leather chair, allowing it to envelope him in a familiar way that seemed to give him an unconscious power. He rested his hands in his lap, and for the first time since she'd arrived relaxed a bit.

Austyn shifted and threw him a stony stare. "That's what you should have asked on Saturday night." After a moment of hesitation, she took a deep breath, closed her eyes, and began, "I keep having this dream. At first, I'm running down this dark alley and my clothes are being ripped from my body by a bunch of faceless men. I hear their voices calling out to me, but I can't make out what they're saying. I just keep running. Then the dream shifts and I'm in this large room, involved in explicit sexual acts with strange men."

Austyn moaned and cupped her breasts.

Donathan was taken aback. He was unsure whether she was serious or if this was a part of her sick game. He picked up his notepad from the side table and decided to play along, as if he were talking to one of his patients.

"Is there anyone you recognize in these dreams?"

He watched her brow furrow while she tumbled through her thoughts, recounting the details of her story in her head.

"I-I don't know. There's also a woman . . . I can hear her laughing at me, but I can't see who she is. She's trying to punish me." Austyn whimpered, tiny beads of sweat now visible on her forehead.

It was hard for him to stay focused. On one hand, he wanted to psychoanalyze her, but flashes of the naked pictures she'd sent to him made Donathan cringe. All he wanted to do was wrap his fingers around her neck and choke the shit out of her, but he didn't, simply because he knew it wouldn't do a bit of good. He had to find out what she wanted from him and give it to her so he could get those pictures. He continued to play along a bit to see where it might lead him.

He cleared his throat. "Who's trying to punish you?"

"I-I don't know who she is," Austyn stammered, fear evident in her voice. "She's been after me since I was twelve."

"Who has been after you?" he questioned, the professional in him telling him her confessions were sounding more like real trauma and not made up, as he'd thought a few minutes before.

"I told you, I don't know. When the dreams first started, I used to fight and scream more when the men were touching me, but as I've grown older, I've hungered for them."

Donathan scanned his mental Rolodex, trying to find any similarities from previous cases that resembled this situation. He drew a blank. He'd seen instances where young women acted out sexually when they'd been raped, but he wasn't sure yet if that was the case with Austyn.

Everything about her was tense now. Her fidgeting fingers twisted the hem of her black skirt, drawing attention to her slender bare legs, which were now crossed at the ankles. She had only been in his office for ten minutes and he could tell there was a lot going on. He scribbled again on his notepad, observed her face, which was twisted, as if she was having an out-of-body experience.

"Why are these dreams a problem for you now, Austyn?"

She shifted slightly on the couch. "They're raping me," she said, jumping to her feet. "And I like it."

Donathan was stunned into silence. This was a different woman, he realized, from the confident one who'd sauntered into his office a few minutes earlier. Suddenly, Austyn grabbed her purse off the table and bolted for the door.

Donathan stood abruptly, knocking over the vase of fresh flowers, the water spewing onto the floor. "Austyn, wait." As she rushed out of his office, he abandoned the flowers and followed after her. He reached the parking lot in time to see a silver-blue Saturn speeding away.

"Damn it!" he yelled in frustration before retreating back to his office. When he entered the reception area, Elaine handed him an envelope.

"Dr. James, Ms. Greene left this for you." His heart stopped as he reached for the familiar courier envelope, praying it was unopened. He clutched the envelope, looking from his receptionist to the waiting patient.

"Give me a moment." He went into his office and slammed the door. He opened the envelope, more pictures staring back at him. His face still wasn't visible, but Sydney would know his naked body. All he'd thought about for the past three days was finding Austyn and she'd shown up on his doorstep, but nothing had changed. He needed to talk to somebody.

He reached into his desk drawer, retrieved his phone, and texted Tony a message.

Meet me at the Ozumo @ 6.

If Austyn was planning to blackmail him, he was going to need a plan. And if anyone could help him come up with that, Tony could.

CHAPTER 13

Sydney arrived in Chicago without incident. She leaned back into the leather seat of the luxury sedan and looked out the window at the mass of navy-blue water extending for an eternity. She spotted the running path along the water's edge.

The driver steered the car in front of the W Hotel on Lake Shore Drive. Engine shut off, the driver appeared at the back door of the sedan and assisted Sydney as she stepped onto the pavement.

She hurried through the double doors to the check-in counter, took her room key, crossed the lobby, which reminded her of a chic living room, and stepped into the elevator. Before the doors closed, her iPhone jingled. She fumbled around, then fished it from the bottom of her bag and, without looking at the screen, answered it.

"Hey, sexy," Donathan said, his coos of affection dancing through the phone.

"Hey," she answered, her response short and as lifeless as she felt.

"Have you checked into your hotel yet?" His words faded in and out due to the weak signal.

"I'm in the elevator."

"I miss you."

As she watched the numbers creep upward, Sydney let his

words hang in the air. She didn't want to say what she was think-ing: he was flat-out lying.

"Sydney? Sydney? I can't hear you," he said before the call dropped.

The elevator opened on the tenth floor and she marched along the wide, bright hallway to her room, which was about halfway down the corridor. She couldn't believe Donathan had the nerve to let the word *miss* come out of his mouth. He must have fallen and hit his head if he thought a simple *I miss you* was going to ex-cuse his behavior over the past few days. He needed a taste of his own medicine. But what she needed right now was some food and some stress relief, and she knew where to get both.

No sooner had she closed her door behind her, the bellman delivered her luggage. She changed into her running tights, laced up her Saucony running shoes, and was nearly out the door when her phone buzzed again. She hesitated at the door, then let it close behind her. She was always at the mercy of her phone; this time she decided whoever was on the other end of the line could wait.

"Damn it," Donathan yelled, tossing his iPhone onto the pas-senger seat. That conversation with Sydney had not gone as he'd planned. He wanted to end the tension and smooth things over, not make them worse, which is what he had a feeling he'd done.

He was speeding down I-24 on his way to an STD clinic in Concord and shook his head at the irony. A split-second image of himself, naked with Austyn straddling him, flashed through his mind. He had to get out of Oakland; he had no idea who he would bump into, including patients or one of Sydney's friends.

By the time Donathan parked behind the Stanwell Circle building, he was tired. The hours he'd been keeping over the past few days were catching up with him and his energy was low. When he stepped out of the car, he noticed the parking lot was empty. That meant the clinic wasn't busy. He hoped to get in and out and back to Oakland in time to meet Tony by six.

Once inside the single-story building, Donathan signed in, using a fake name he'd concocted, all the while thinking about what would happen if Sydney got wind of him being there. She would leave his ass in a hot second without asking any questions.

"Raynard Dodson," the medical assistant called out.

Donathan didn't move the first time, but the second time the young woman called out the name, the alias registered, and she gave him a knowing smirk as he stood and moved toward her. At first he was nervous about his reaction, but the closer he got to her, the more his demeanor changed. Hell, this was an STD clinic, he thought; he was certain people gave aliases all the time.

A little more than two hours later, and clear of things you could instantly check under a microscope, Donathan sat with Tony at a table in the back of Ozumo. A few seconds had passed since he'd pushed two identical envelopes across the table.

"You all right, man?" Tony asked, never taking his eyes off Donathan as he removed his brown jacket and loosely draped it on the back of his chair. Donathan leaned back and stared at the envelopes. He was tired of people asking him that and no, he wasn't all right; he wouldn't be until he got the results back from the HIV and other STD tests he'd just taken and figured out what to do about the situation contained in the envelopes.

Tony took a swig of his Heineken, scooped up the envelopes one at a time, and reviewed the contents. He looked at Donathan and grimaced.

"Man, what the fuck is this? Please tell me that's not you."

Donathan shrugged. The anxiety he'd lived with for the past few days was now back sitting on his chest.

He stabbed the envelopes with his index finger like he was killing someone. "That's the chick from the golf course."

"I knew she was bad news when I laid eyes on her—"

"She showed up at Maxwell's, we talked, we had a drink, one thing led to another, and I woke up tied to the bed in her hotel room—"

"Tied to a bed in a hotel? What the fuck?"

"Man, keep your voice down." Donathan looked around to make sure no one had overheard Tony's last comment.

"I thought Sydney was going to Maxwell's with you."

"She was supposed to, but she got called in to the hospital. Long story short, when I left the hotel room I couldn't find my wallet, but by the time I got home, that crazy bitch had left it at my house. On Monday she dropped off the first envelope, then she had the nerve to show up at my office today and give me the other one. To top it all off, I think the bitch is nuts."

"No shit, Sherlock. Any woman who would go to these lengths after fucking you one time isn't wrapped too tight."

"That's true, but I really believe she is mentally unstable. When she came to the office today, she was acting cool and in control. But within fifteen minutes she'd completely unraveled, raved that some men had raped her in her dreams, then stormed out. I went after her, but by the time I got to the parking lot she was gone."

"Man, this is some fucked-up shit."

"I know. I've racked my brain for the last four days, trying to figure out what to do, but with Sydney breathing down my neck, I couldn't maneuver like I needed to. Now she's out of town for a few days and I need to get a handle on this before she gets back."

"Who is the crazy woman, anyway?"

"All I know about her is her name and the phone number listed on the business card she left on my car window," Donathan said, concerned for the first time that the name on the card could be an alias just like the one he'd given at the STD clinic.

"Have you thought about hiring a private investigator?" Tony reached into his wallet and sifted through some business cards until he located the one he wanted. "Here, I picked this up at one of the law offices on my route months ago. I'd thought about hiring him to locate my pops..."

Donathan brushed the pad of his thumb across the raised letters on the worn card. *Curtis Holsey, Private Investigator.* Donathan and Tony had been friends for decades and had exorcised many demons together, including Tony's father, who played a recurring role in many of their exorcisms.

Out of the blue, a young woman approached their table. She was wearing a lime-green minidress that was so short Donathan could see the daisy pattern on her panty with every step she took toward him. "Excuse me. I hate to bother you, but can I please get your autograph for my mother? Her name is Linda and she's a huge fan," she squealed as she bounced up and down. Her perky breasts kept time with her movements. She handed Donathan a piece of paper and he quickly scribbled his name and handed the paper back. Donathan's eyes squeezed her tits and caressed her ass as she walked away.

"Now see, it's that right there that got your ass in trouble in the first place," Tony said, looking at his watch. "It's too late now, but I think you should give Curtis Holsey a call tomorrow. In the meantime, quit looking at that girl like you want to season and eat her."

Donathan looked back at Tony and laughed for the first time in days. Tony was right. When Sydney was out of town, his usual agenda was to fuck for sport, but right now he needed some self-control. He took another fleeting look at the girl and then sighed heavily.

"Man, looking ain't hurt nobody, but right now, if it ain't my own, I don't want anything to do with pussy."

Chapter 14

Miles Day reminded Sydney of Denzel Washington as he glided across the hotel lobby. His dark jeans hung low at his waist and his brown-and-baby-blue–pinstripe button-down shirt contrasted sharply with the hue of his skin. When Sydney's eyes reached his shoes, she grinned at the shined dark brown gators. *Chicago* looked sexy and damn good.

Her smile quickly faded and she scolded herself for her thoughts as he approached her. It was six-fifteen exactly and he was there to pick her up for the game. When the server appeared, she instructed him to charge the bill to her room.

Miles noticed the empty plate in front of her. "I hope you got my message and didn't eat anything."

"I didn't get your message until a few minutes ago. But I didn't eat much."

They walked across the shiny marbled floor, out the revolving door, and hopped into the midnight-blue GMC Yukon parked along the circular drive. Seat belt buckled, Sydney turned to face Miles.

The husky voice of José James soothed her. "So, tell me what you've been doing for the past few days."

"Not much...had a sleepover with my daughters. Yesterday I took them to the American Girl store on Michigan Avenue. Their dolls had hair appointments, needed some new clothes, and we had tea."

"Sounds like you had your hands full."

"Yes, I did, but I enjoyed every minute of it. I don't get to spend much time with them since I left Chicago. The distance is killing me, but thanks to FaceTime, webcams, and Skype, I get to say good morning to them on most days, and I read bedtime stories to them every other night."

His cell phone rang; he adjusted the music volume, then reached above his head and pressed an illuminated blue button on a flat black speaker the size of the palm of his hand.

"Hello?"

"Daddy," the tiny voice whined into the confines of the car. "You forgot to read me a bedtime story." Sydney studied him and smiled.

"Sweetheart, Mommy is reading you a story tonight. Remember Daddy read the story last night."

"But I like it when you read to me, Daddy."

"Tell you what Daddy is going to do. Tomorrow night I'll read you two stories, okay?"

"But I want you to read me a story tonight. Can you come over—?"

The conversation with his daughter was cut short when a woman's voice came booming over the line.

"So, are you coming over to read her a bedtime story?"

"Stephanie, my coming over wasn't part of our agreement—"

"Miles, it's not like you see them every day, and if all your daughter wants is for you to read her a story in person, then I don't see what the problem is."

"Look, Stephanie, you heard me tell the girls when I dropped them off a few hours ago that I would see tomorrow. It was never a part of the plan for me to come back to read to them tonight and now isn't a good time to discuss this."

"It's never a good time to discuss a damn thing with you. Your shit is tired, Miles, and I'm sick of it."

Sydney looked away. She could see the United Center in the distance and was fascinated that it looked like they'd erected it right in the middle of the hood. She heard Miles blow out a ragged breath before he continued. "We'll talk about this later, Stephanie. Kiss Arielle and tell her I'll see her tomorrow."

"Well, I hope whatever bitch you're wooing is worth it. You don't get to see them that much and now you're too damn busy to read her a bedtime story. Maybe I need to find her another daddy who will." A deafening dial tone followed.

Miles's jaw tightened as he wheeled the Yukon into the parking lot of the arena. He flashed their tickets to the parking attendant and was directed toward the VIP lot. After he parked, Miles turned off the engine and sat motionless for a moment. He was so deep in thought, it seemed like he'd forgotten Sydney was there.

"I'm sorry you had to hear that."

"No big deal. I imagine coparenting can be tough."

"You don't know the half of it. I'm so tired of fighting with Stephanie over things that don't make sense. I've been here for three days and every single day we've argued about something."

"It sounds like she's angry with you and hasn't quite embraced her feelings about the divorce."

"I know. It's been a year and I try to give her the space to do that, but she constantly uses our children as chess pieces in her games. I try to keep the peace for their sake, but that venom she spewed just now had nothing to do with my daughters."

"Oh, that was very clear."

"I wouldn't trade my daughters for anything in the world, but it's times like these when I wish I had listened to my mother. We got married when I was thirty-two and now, at forty-two, I have to deal with this drama."

It was almost game time and the United Center was crawling with thousands of fans, piling in to see the Chicago Bulls. Sydney and Miles exited the car into the brisk evening air and stopped to admire the Michael Jordan statue in front of the arena. After taking a few pictures, they entered through the row of glass doors and came face-to-face with Benny the Bull, the infamous team mascot who was doing what he did best: pumping up the crowd.

A glass of wine awaited them as they were the first to be escorted into the private skybox, where she learned that Miles's brothers were the season occupants. Sydney took the glass, nestled into one of the plush leather seats, and enjoyed the game and Miles's family reunion.

During the fourth quarter, the game was winding down and Miles took a seat beside her. "That's like the fifth time your phone has rung. Aren't you going to answer it?"

Sydney blushed, a little embarrassed because she'd been busted. She'd purposely placed her ringer on low and thought with all the excitement she was the only one aware of the multiple jingles she'd chosen to ignore throughout the game.

"No, I'm not."

"Well, is everything okay?"

"Everything is great."

As they headed to the car, Sydney thought back to the earlier telephone conversation she'd overheard between Miles and his ex-wife. The woman on the other end of the line had sounded desperate and evil. Miles, on the other hand, seemed like a really nice guy who didn't deserve to have someone talk to him like his ex-wife had. Sydney knew there were always two sides to every story. Was there something about Miles she couldn't see? Something he was hiding?

As Miles pulled away from the United Center, traffic snaked along. Once outside the parking lot, he made a sharp turn onto a side street, then glanced over at Sydney, who seemed a little uncomfortable with her surroundings. He patted her shoulder.

"Don't worry, I know where I'm going."

"It's a good thing you do. Wouldn't want to get jacked in the hood."

A few minutes later Miles parallel parked next to a building.

"Where are we?"

"Well, we didn't get to have dinner, so I thought we could do dessert."

Aware of the late hour, Sydney knew she would regret this to-morrow, when the two-hour time difference caught up with her. "This had better be good."

The pair entered the Wine Tasting Room and were escorted to a set of narrow wooden stairs in the back of the building. The stairs led to a spacious second floor with cozy chairs, love seats, and sofas scattered in intimate settings. Vintage art adorned the walls and votive candles perched on the coffee tables gave the room a soft, warm glow. Miles directed her to a secluded love seat and or-dered two glasses of Viognier and the Wine Tasting Room's signature chocolate fondue. She sat down and fought the urge to remove her spike-heeled shoes.

"So what did you think about the United Center?" Miles asked.

"I enjoyed it tremendously. Between watching you, your brothers, and Benny the Bull, I had a wonderful time."

"Me and my brothers?"

"I found your interactions so refreshing. You see, I'm an only child. I always wished for a brother or sister to share my space. It was really cool watching the bond between you. Oh, and the game was good, too."

"I guess it's evident that I love my family. I just wish my girls would get to experience that bond more. Since I moved to Cali-fornia, they've only visited my parents twice. Stephanie isn't real big on my family."

The server returned with the wine and fondue and they skirted around the nasty telephone conversation, but the glass of wine Sydney had promised herself she wouldn't have before they'd come in was the liquid courage she needed to introduce the subject head-on.

"So, tell me about Stephanie." Sydney assumed he'd be as free with this information as he'd been with all her previous questions, but to her surprise, Miles got real quiet. A silence hung over them, and Sydney wondered if she should have mentioned Stephanie after all. "Miles, I'm sorry. That was an inappropriate question.

Your ex-wife is none of my business, and asking about her was really out of place."

"Thank you for trying to be polite, but I'm a big boy and I'm not afraid of hard questions."

"Well, you did get kind of quiet there. Just making sure I didn't overstep my bounds."

"The question was fine. I was quiet because I was trying to think of something nice to say," he said, leaning back into the love seat. "Give me your feet."

"My feet?" It was as if he had read her mind. The wine had her on autopilot and the six miles she'd run earlier had her feet aching for a rub. She bit into a chocolate-dipped strawberry, removed her shoes, and placed her feet in his lap as requested.

"Oooh." His firm hands sent shockwaves through her body. She picked up the wineglass, took a sip, and swallowed a moan. His hands felt so good. For the next fifteen minutes Sydney closed her eyes and moaned as Miles caressed and kneaded. The voice of the waitress yanked her from her euphoric enjoyment.

"Would you like another glass of wine?"

Sydney quickly removed her feet from Miles's lap, but not before they brushed against the bulge that pressed hard against his pants. She avoided eye contact with him. "No, I think I've had enough."

Chapter 15

When Payton returned to her condo after her seven p.m. Fit Body workout, she showered, pulled on some shorts and a T-shirt, ate a bowl of pasta, and then checked her email for the first time in a few days. Her in-box was overflowing with messages from the PerfectChemistry.com dating service. The one that read *Let the sparks fly 4 free* stood out. Free her ass.

"Ugh." She shuddered at the memory of her last date. This little experience had been expensive. She only had a few more dates to go to get her refund, but she decided then and there the nuisance of going out with a bunch of losers wasn't worth it. Besides, Tony was occupying a lot of her free time and their little arrangement was working out just fine.

She fished her cell phone from her gym bag, wondering if he would call tonight, but her cheeks deflated when she saw that her battery was dead.

"Shit."

As soon as she plugged it in, she noted multiple missed calls: three from Tony and one from Sydney, whom she hadn't spoken to since the Copia event. It was almost midnight in Chicago, but she dialed anyway and was a little surprised when Sydney answered on the first ring.

"Hey, girl," Payton sang. "What's got you up this late in the Windy City?"

"I just got in from the game not long ago."

"So how was it?"

"How was what?"

"The Bulls game?" Payton was confused by the slight edge of defensiveness she detected in Sydney's voice.

"The game was great. Miles and the Day clan were the perfect hosts."

"Are the brothers as fine as Miles?"

"Absolutely. They were all lovely."

"Lovely? Sydney, if the brothers look anything like Miles, the last word I'd use to describe them would be lovely. What the hell is wrong with you?"

"Nothing is wrong with me."

Payton wasn't convinced. "You know I'm not good at this type of stuff, but if you want to talk about it . . ." Payton hoped Sydney wouldn't take her up on the offer. She really wasn't in the mood to hear about whatever it was that was bothering Sydney and now wished she'd returned Tony's call first.

"Payton, you and I both know you don't really want to hear me talk about my problems."

"Well, I know something is bothering you and you'd better take advantage of my offer to listen. Otherwise, you'll probably need some Botox injections."

Sydney raised her hand to touch her forehead, her frown deepening more.

"Going once. Going twice—"

"Okay, okay, okay . . . I . . . um . . . Donathan and I aren't getting along."

"What did Inspector Gadget do this time?" Payton referred to Donathan by the nickname she had given him because on so many occasions he was tinkering with something electronic and technical and had numerous remote controls to prove it.

"He's been acting strange since Sunday—"

"I thought Brea told me he wasn't feeling well?"

"I thought that was the problem initially, but now I'm not so sure. He may just be acting out because I was called into the hospital and couldn't attend a promotional event for the radio station with him last Saturday night."

"Well, has he said anything about your not going?"

"No, he hasn't said much of anything. First he sulked around the bedroom for two days and today he did a disappearing act on me."

"What do you mean, a disappearing act?"

"He left the house today before I got up and he knew I was going out of town. He's never done that before."

"Are you on your period or something, because nothing you've told me sounds all that strange?"

"But that's not all. He had the nerve to call me earlier today and tell me he missed me. But before I left, he was acting like I had the plague or something." Sydney's voice quivered as she swallowed her anger.

Payton laughed out loud.

"What the hell are you laughing at?"

"I think I see what your problem is and I know exactly how you can fix it. Get up and walk over to your carry-on bag, grab your vibrator, do yourself, and take your ass to sleep."

"This isn't about sex, Payton."

"Um, I beg to differ. It sounds like the inspector's deprivation has left you fuckstrated. I hope your mood was better at the game."

The mention of the game caused Sydney to hesitate before she responded. "Fuckstrated? Is that even a word?"

"You know exactly what I'm talking about. Sydney, don't go making this more than it is. Look, just because you guys had a few off days sexually, stop being a bitch about it and call the man so y'all can kiss and make up. Now I have to run, but call me with an update tomorrow."

Speechless, it took Sydney a few minutes to process the call that had just ended. She couldn't believe Payton, of all people, was coming to Donathan's defense. But the advice made sense. She fell back on the bed into the fluffy pillows and imagined how Donathan would react if her behavior had mirrored his. He would have a fit. She noticed it was almost eleven o'clock in El Cerrito, and no matter how she was feeling about his bad behavior, it didn't warrant more bad behavior on her part.

Sydney quickly dialed her home number. When the voice mail picked up, her anger resurfaced. She wanted so desperately to believe that the problem was nothing more than Donathan feeling a little under the weather, but she had been with this man for ten years and her gut instinct told her differently. Something was definitely going on with Donathan. She willed herself not to call his cell phone, but on impulse she texted him:

Where the hell are you?

Apparently, his ass wasn't *that* sick or he would be at home in bed at this time of night. She closed her eyes and reached for calm. As she tossed her cell phone on the nightstand, she caught sight of her Bulls ticket stub and was flooded with a flashback of Miles rubbing her feet. Simply thinking about him made her nipples pucker and she panicked as guilt washed over her. She couldn't understand why she was all of a sudden so intrigued by this man.

Switching gears, she picked the Eric Jerome Dickey novel up off the nightstand and immersed herself in the sexually charged tale. She might not have been having sex tonight, but thanks to the author, at least somebody was.

Chapter 16

When Donathan arrived at Alta Bates Summit Medical Center, he was relieved to find Tony seated in the critical care waiting room. "What happened? Is she all right?"

Donathan had been home only a few hours when he'd received Tony's frantic telephone call. He was so worried, he'd rushed out the door without his cell phone.

Tony looked up and sighed with resignation. "When I got home, she was having trouble breathing. And you know my mom...always trying to take care of someone else but not wanting people to take care of her. Man, she's so stubborn she didn't even want me to call nine-one-one."

"Is she all right?" Donathan repeated, praying not to hear any bad news. Shirley Barnes was a second mother to him.

"Yeah, she's resting comfortably now. Turns out she was having a reaction to the chemotherapy. The doctor told me to go home because she's going to be out of it for the rest of the night, but you know I can't do that. I...I just need to go get my wheels."

Donathan could see the struggle etched on Tony's face. They sat in silence for a long moment. Like his friend, Donathan, too, was trying to accept the fact that Shirley Barnes was dying and there was nothing he could do or say to change that.

"What about Najee?" Donathan asked. "Sydney will be back in a few days. Maybe she can come to stay with us for a while."

"My aunt Rosemary is at the house taking good care of her. I don't know what I'd have done if she hadn't come out here to help me through this."

At that moment Donathan realized he'd been a fucked-up friend. Every conversation he'd had with Tony over the past few days had been focused on himself. Donathan was so troubled by all the nonsense affecting his life that he'd forgotten that his best friend needed him. He knew he was dealing with his own shit, but he vowed to do better.

"Wait right here. I'll be back."

Donathan left the waiting room, headed toward the double doors at the end of the hallway, and picked up the wall phone. He announced himself to the nurse, and the loud click of the releasing lock prompted him to pull the heavy door open. The smell of sickness slapped him in the face. He entered Shirley Barnes's room and found her resting as Tony had said she would be. He walked over to the bed and stared down at her for a long time before he touched her arm. She opened her eyes and stared up at him.

"Donathan, is that you, baby?"

"Yes, ma'am, it's me," he said softly.

"Don't look so pitiful, baby. I'm going to be just fine. But I need you to promise me you'll look after Tony. Can you do that for me, baby?" she questioned. Her eyes fluttered as she teetered on the edge of peaceful slumber.

Tears filled his eyes and slowly rolled down his cheeks. He wiped them away before he kissed her on the forehead.

"Yes, ma'am. I can do that."

Chapter 17

It was almost three o'clock in the afternoon and Joi sat at Tyrese's desk in his home office, staring at the computer screen. She'd just called Holsey Investigations just as she had every day since their initial meeting and the detective still had no information for her. She decided it was time to take matters into her own hands. She typed *cheating husband* into the Google toolbar and waited for the list to populate the screen.

Joi scanned the list of sites and clicked on the link to "How to trap your lying, cheating husband." She removed the small moleskin journal from her purse and opened it to the pages where she had been keeping track of Tyrese's suspicious activities and taking notes. The site suggested she track his car mileage, credit card statements, ATM withdrawals, and phone records, all things she never paid any attention to, especially those having to do with money because Tyrese paid all the bills. Joi sighed. How did she get into this situation?

A flashing advertisement caught her attention. *No Matter What or Who You Want to Track, We Have the Right Solution for Any Situation.* She double-clicked on the link that took her to Ironclad Security. The page was filled with rows and rows of tiny GPS tracking devices in all shapes, sizes, and colors. Overwhelmed by so many to choose from, Joi clicked on the Livewire FastTrac, the internet special of the week.

The device looked tiny, like it could fit into the palm of her hand. It had a battery life of up to ten days and provided real-time tracking with ten-second updates. She smiled briefly at the thought that this might be the answer to her prayers, but the smile quickly turned into a frown when she read the description and realized the device cost $399.95 plus $69.95 for activation and $39.95 for a one-month subscription.

Uneasy, Joi removed her new credit card from her wallet and stared at it. She had never applied for a credit card in her name before and couldn't believe how fast she had been approved. Now the plastic was burning a hole in her purse.

Joi had grown up in the projects of North Richmond. When she and her twin brother, Justin, were fourteen, the success of multiple real estate transactions had catapulted their family to a new financial status. She and Justin were thrust into the good life and the best private schools the Bay Area had to offer. Then, during her freshman year of college at UC Berkeley, her father had been murdered. Some said a disgruntled employee had killed him; others maintained it was his shady business dealings had killed him. Either way, the father who'd worked hard to provide for his family was replaced with a single mother trying not to end up back in the projects. And Joi certainly didn't want to end up back there. She and Tyrese lived in an upscale neighborhood in the type of home she had grown accustomed to for herself and her children. If she did divorce Tyrese, she had to make sure the payout would be worth it. Whatever happened with her marriage, she had to make sure her children wouldn't suffer for the sins of their father. She looked at the price of the tracking device plus the extra shipping cost for overnight delivery and clicked the Buy Now button. No amount of money was too much to get to the bottom of this.

Joi cleared the computer history and shut it down. She grabbed her purse off the desk and headed out to pick up her boys from playgroup. For the first time in weeks she felt like she was moving in the right direction. She had a feeling that being able to track Tyrese's exact whereabouts twenty-four hours a day would definitely come in handy.

★ ★ ★

Donathan hesitated in the office doorway. He watched Tyrese's long fingers dance across the computer keyboard, then stepped into the office, leaving the door slightly ajar. He stopped at the minirefrigerator and grabbed a bottle of water before taking a seat. When he looked up, a pair of piercing gray eyes were fixed on him.

"I think I need to fire my secretary," Tyrese said, peering over the top of his laptop docking station. "What are you doing in my neck of the woods?"

"I was in the neighborhood," Donathan answered nonchalantly. But he knew the Oracle Arena was not someplace you just happened by. Tyrese usually worked downtown at the Warrior corporate offices, but due to some special project, he'd been relocated to the coliseum for the past few months.

Donathan was on that side of town because he had agreed to meet Holsey, the private investigator, at the strip mall on Hegenberger across the freeway and needed to pass a little time before his four o'clock meeting.

"Man, that's bullshit and you know it, especially because my office is in the middle of East Oakland." Donathan waited for the usual smile that came after a playful jab like that, but it never came.

"Did I catch you at a bad time?"

Tyrese sighed. "Nope. I have a meeting in twenty minutes—"

Donathan stood. "All right, man. I didn't mean to barge in on you—"

"Man, sit your ass down. You're not barging in on me."

"Seriously, I'll catch up with you later."

"Actually, you came at the right time because I need some logic to figure out this damn mess I've created."

Donathan sat back down in the leather chair and waited.

"Well, it happened last week. I was working with one of our new temps after-hours, things got out of hand, and bodily fluids were exchanged. Ever since then, she keeps requesting—or shall I say almost threatening—that I meet her outside of work or she might have to tell somebody about our little physical encounter."

"Have you met with her outside of work yet?"

"No. I mean, I'm not exactly sure of her angle, but I'm tired of her innuendos, so I scheduled a meeting with her at four o'clock today to feel her out. This could be disastrous."

For the first time Tyrese noticed the slight crack in the door and he jumped up to close it. He leaned his six-foot-seven frame against the corner of his desk and looked down at Donathan, who was devoid of any emotion.

Donathan had met Tyrese at a barbershop over seven years before and they'd become fast friends, yet for some reason he hadn't told Tyrese about his latest debauchery: Austyn.

"I could lose my job behind this dumb shit and how would I explain that to Joi?"

"What are you, retarded or something? Please tell me you used a condom."

"Of course I did. I may have faltered in judgment, but I'm not a damn fool."

"I'm not so sure about the last part, but at least she won't show up at your door a few months from now, talking about she's pregnant."

Tyrese rubbed his open palm across his bald head, another one of his attributes that drove women crazy. "Not unless swallowing my seed could knock her up."

"Okay, so what's the worst thing she could say? From where I sit it sounds like you have the upper hand. It's your word against hers. It's not like you forced her or anything—"

"Hell no. She was a willing participant, and damn good at it," he said, picking up a picture of his sons from his desk.

Donathan shook his head. "Ty, man, you're slipping. You are *never* supposed to mix business and pleasure."

"Well, shit, like you just said, nobody can prove anything."

"I just don't want to have to bail you out if the girl cries rape."

Tyrese looked on, bewildered by Donathan's comments. "Man, I don't really know this girl. I mean, she's only been working here for about a month, and if she decides to cry sexual harassment, my ass is grass."

Donathan stared at his friend. Normally, he would chalk Tyrese's little indiscretion up to inexperience and advise him to learn from his mistake and move on. But because of what he himself was going through with Austyn, he was beginning to believe his own carelessness and know-it-all attitude was what had gotten him into this mess. He was always careful and he never let these women get too close, which was why Austyn unnerved him so. She'd been to his house, his office, forced her way into his private space, and there was nothing he could do about it. He and Tyrese were cut from the same cloth and it had always been: He who got the most panties won the game. He felt like such a hypocrite; his situation was ten times worse than Tyrese's. He couldn't think of any way to prevent his friend from traveling the road of private detectives and STD clinics. He looked at his watch, rose from his chair, and moved toward the door.

"I'm about to be late for my appointment. In the meantime, let's just hope the girl doesn't have a big mouth and dollar signs for eyes."

Tyrese looked uneasy. "That's exactly why I scheduled our little meeting."

Donathan rushed to his car. The unsettled feeling he'd had in the pit of his stomach earlier now permeated his entire body. He couldn't wait to meet with the private detective. He had to get the scoop on Austyn. There was too much riding on it not to.

He arrived at a strip mall, scanned the parking aisles for the light blue Toyota Corolla, and felt disappointed when he didn't see it. He wanted to get Austyn Greene off his back and his life back to the way things used to be. He turned into an open parking space and retrieved the white letter-sized envelope from his glove box. Once the envelope was folded and tucked neatly in his breast pocket, he stepped out of the car and scanned the lot a second time. There was no Holsey to be seen. Cussing under his breath, he decided to run into the store to pick up some water. He'd been feeling dehydrated since Sunday and had concluded it had something to do with whatever Austyn had given him to make him more susceptible to her plan.

The light blue Toyota pulled up and honked just as he was about to enter the front doors of Starbucks. Startled, Donathan turned to see the culprit. For a moment he hesitated, wondering if he should enter the coffee bar or retreat back toward the car. Why the hell would this dude come blazing into the parking lot, honking his horn? The last thing he needed right now was attention. He looked around once more and headed in the direction of the vehicle.

Chapter 18

Instead of paying attention to the discussion on pediatric brain injury, Sydney's mind drifted. She'd managed to avoid Miles all day today, until now. The subtle smell of his cologne and the tiny pinpricks that cursed through her every time his arm brushed against hers made her nipples stand at attention.

She buttoned her suit jacket to hide the evidence and gathered her laptop from the conference table, folding it into her tote bag.

"Where are you going?" he whispered into her ear, his facial hair gently grazing the side of Sydney's face. She sat up straighter. It was almost five o'clock in the afternoon and workshops were almost over for the day.

"Back to my hotel," she said, leaning away from the contact. She stood and he followed as she led the way toward the door.

"Aren't you going to the mixer?" he asked, once they'd stepped into the lobby and the conference-room doors had closed behind them.

"Yes, but I need to drop off some things and make a few phone calls," she said, happy that she was now far enough away from Miles to inhale some sobering oxygen.

"I have a two-room suite and there's more than enough space up there for you to make yourself comfortable—"

"Miles, that's very sweet of you, but that won't be necessary. My hotel is just up the block—"

"I know exactly where your hotel is, but it doesn't make sense for you to go back and forth when you can go upstairs. There's even a separate bathroom if you need it." He retrieved the key card from his wallet and extended it in her direction.

Sydney looked up at him, her gaze fused with his.

"You go on up and make yourself comfortable. I'm going to check out the vendors, and then I promised Julia I'd have a drink with her."

Sydney computed her options. She'd been hesitant about accepting his offer, before, but if he was having drinks with Julia she knew he'd be occupied for hours.

"Y'know what, I think I'll take you up on your generous offer." She smiled and accepted his room key. "All I need is about an hour."

By the time the clear glass box reached the twenty-second floor, a wave of doubt rested in the pit of Sydney's stomach. Had she made the right decision in accepting a man's room key? She looked left and right as she made her way to room 2224, where she pushed the key card into the slot and pulled it out again. When the small light turned green, she stepped inside. Why was she nervous? Miles hadn't done anything other than be a perfect gentleman. She pondered her question a bit longer before accepting what she knew to be true. It wasn't Miles who was making her uneasy.

She rested her tote bag on a faux antique chair and maneuvered into the spacious sitting area of the suite. She was immediately drawn to the wall of windows with breathtaking, unobstructed views of the city. She lingered a moment, then walked into the master suite, stealing a peek into Miles's world. His toiletries were perched neatly on the granite vanity next to his black leather bag, and his razor, soap, and toothbrush cases were all black and matched perfectly.

"I knew he was a neat freak," she said out loud, before making her way back to the sitting area, which was almost as big as her entire hotel room at the W Hotel.

She plopped down on the sage-green couch and said with an exhausted sigh, "I could sure use another foot rub right now." She switched on the television, found the smooth jazz music station, and melted into the sofa as the scent of Miles's cologne teased the fringes of her mind. For the first time she decided to admit to herself that she enjoyed seeing and talking to him. She fantasized about his strong hands kneading her feet briefly before the guilt set in, then she took out her cell phone and dialed Donathan. He picked up, but a few seconds passed before she finally heard his voice.

"Baby, I'm in the middle of something, I have to call you right back."

"Where are you?" Sydney asked, relieved that he'd finally answered the phone but curious about his hastiness. "Is everything all right?"

Voice low, he replied, "Everything's fine. Why wouldn't it be?"

"We've been missing each other and I just wanted to make sure you were okay. I mean, we haven't—"

"Syd, I have to go. I promise I'll call you right back." Before she could say another word, he ended the call.

Sydney was pissed. She couldn't believe he'd practically hung up on her. Donathan should have been kissing her ass, not hanging up on her. They hadn't had one complete conversation since she'd left California and frankly, she was tired of it.

When Miles entered the suite, he found Sydney curled up in the fetal position on the sofa. It had been over an hour since she'd gone upstairs, and when she hadn't reappeared downstairs as she'd indicated she would, he'd decided to go check on her. Seeing her peaceful and unguarded, he found himself unable to do anything but stare at her. Unlike yesterday, when her hair had been bone straight, today it was a wavy mass, covering most of her face. The hem of her skirt rested at midthigh, showing off her shapely runner's legs. She was even more beautiful sleeping, and he was just as enchanted with her today as he was last night. After the game he hadn't wanted to drop her off at her hotel, but once he had he'd lain in bed for hours, mentally trying to put everything into perspective. Sydney was a beautiful woman but, most importantly, she was married and should have been off limits to him. But he could feel she wasn't.

By choice, he hadn't had sex since he'd moved to California months earlier, when he'd promised himself to break the dysfunctional cycle of continuing to have sex with his ex-wife. This was his first trip back to Chicago since then, and after Stephanie's behavior last night, he understood why it had been easier to just have sex with her than to walk through her minefield of vindictive artillery. Sex with her was good. It was familiar, and the ultimate price he paid to see his daughters with as little drama as possible. But what distance had taught Miles was that when all was said and done, sex never changed the fact that their relationship just didn't work, and for the sake of all involved, he knew he had to let that part of their relationship go.

His phone rang and his shoulders tensed as he saw the familiar number dance across the screen. His thoughts had conjured her up. What did Stephanie want now? He hesitated before he answered, praying her call wouldn't be a repeat of last night's shenanigans.

Sydney hadn't realized she'd dozed off until she was startled by the ringing of a cell phone. She opened her eyes, disoriented, and reached for the device from the coffee table but was taken aback by the sound of a deep baritone voice.

"Wassup?" she heard Miles say from across the room. Her heart rate accelerated as she locked eyes with him. He was leaning against the wet bar, his legs crossed one over the other. She swung her legs to the floor, grabbed her tote bag, and excused herself to the bathroom, closing the door behind her. She squinted at her watch. She'd been asleep for over an hour. She turned on the faucet, splashed some cold water on her face, brushed her teeth with her travel toothbrush, and reapplied lip gloss. She poured a few droplets of olive oil into her hand, rubbed her palms together, and then raked her fingers through her dark brown hair. She finished with a few upward strokes of mascara. "Good as new," she said to her reflection.

Sydney heard a light tap on the door. She opened it to find Miles extending her phone in her direction before he walked away and disappeared into one of the bedrooms.

"Hello," Sydney said, as she moved to the couch to slip into her shoes.

"Who was that?" Donathan fired off.

"That was Miles, the neurosurgeon who works at the hospital with me."

"Why is he answering your phone?"

"Probably out of habit—you know how easy it is to forget when we're on or off."

He hesitated, as if he was entertaining her plausible explanation.

"For a man with limited answers you sure are full of questions this evening. Especially because this is one of the longest conversations I've had with you in days."

"Don't try to make this about me. I'm just trying to understand why another man is answering my wife's phone."

"Doctors always answer one another's phones."

"They do when they're working. Where are you?"

"Excuse me?" Sydney grew agitated at his tone. Out of the corner of her eye, she noticed Miles standing in the far bedroom, looking out of the window. He turned toward her and teased her with a slow, sensual smile. She felt like the room was closing in on her.

"Hello. You're not deaf, are you?"

"I can't believe you're acting like this. Yes, a man answered my phone, but with a plausible explanation. Then again, this is the most attention I've gotten from you in a week, so I guess I should be flattered."

"You still haven't answered my question, Sydney. Where are you?"

"I'm not going to answer it and feed into your nonsense. So, either we change the subject or we end this call."

"But we aren't done with this conversation, Sydney."

"Maybe you're not, but I am. I'll call you later when I get to my hotel."

As she dropped her phone into her tote bag, Miles exited the bedroom, closing the distance between them. "Are you ready to head downstairs?"

He opened the door and waited for Sydney to walk out in front of him. "I'm right behind you."

Chapter 19

Payton waited in the passenger pick-up-and-drop-off area of the Bay Point Bart station for Tony's train to arrive. He had agreed to catch the train and meet her to assist with her eviction problem after she finished her site visit at the Glover House Substance Abuse Treatment facility in Pittsburg.

The contractors were on schedule to complete the repairs on her grandparents' house by the end of next week and she was determined not to let any obstacles get in the way of finalizing the sale of the property.

Payton's stomach dropped as she stared through the windshield at Tony as he exited the station. He was over six feet tall and dressed in jeans, a T-shirt, and running shoes. He was attractive in a lean and lanky kind of way, but his most admirable attribute was that he knew how to use that dick of his. He flashed a wide grin and everything went hazy except for him. Behind closed doors, their relationship was easy; no one to judge, just the two of them acting on what came naturally. But outside, as she watched him take steps that led him closer to her, she felt vulnerable and exposed. She unlocked the door and waited for him to get in.

"Damn, it's hot in Bay Point," he said, locking himself into the seat belt.

"Actually, it's not Bay Point, it's West Pittsburg. A few years back they changed the name to distance themselves from Pittsburg's criminal reputation to attract the suburbanites, but this will always be West Pitt."

Tony smiled.

"I can't believe you were born and raised in Oakland but have never been to the Burg."

To bypass the Highway 4 rush-hour traffic, they chose the less-congested side streets, which led to a back road that divided a distant power plant and marshlands on one side from a development of new homes on the other. They passed empty lots, a rundown motel, and small single-family homes with flat-shingle roofs. Devoid of people, the street reminded Payton of East Oakland before the sun went down and the bad elements peppered every corner. She turned off the main drag.

"Is this the neighborhood you grew up in?" Tony asked.

"Yes," she answered, making another right and then a left before pulling into the familiar driveway. When she got out of the car, she stared at the curb in front of the house. At one time it had been painted a bright fire-engine red, with a vibrant San Francisco 49er logo on the sidewalk. The logo was encircled by the words *49er fans live here*. But over time the logo had faded. Payton smiled, remembering how on Sundays when she was growing up, her grandparents would dress from head to toe in their 49er gear, pile into the Cadillac, and head to Candlestick Park to watch Joe Montana and Jerry Rice.

Tony climbed out of the car.

"So what's the plan?"

"Plan? Are you kidding? There is no plan."

"Tell me again how this woman ended up living in the basement."

"Well, when I decided to sell the house, I knew I couldn't do the repairs and have someone living in it, so my uncle Sheldon moved out immediately. My other uncle, Donald, didn't have a job and had nowhere to go, so I told him he could stay in the basement until we sold the house. Then, with his share of the proceeds,

I'd planned to set him up in an apartment and pay his rent for a year. Two weeks ago my uncle Donald landed in jail on a probation violation and the contractor informed me that a woman was living here. I've been trying to move her out since then."

"I take it she's not handing over her key willingly."

"You got that right. This is my third trip out here and the other two times obviously weren't successful."

"Third time's a charm."

They exited the vehicle and Tony followed Payton through the side gate that appeared to lead into the backyard.

When they reached a door covered by a wrought-iron security gate Payton knocked on the screen. After a few minutes and no answer she removed a set of keys from her jacket pocket and unlocked the door. The stench of rotting food suffocated them. A stained mattress and several plastic bags of clothing and utensils were haphazardly strewn on the floor.

"This shit is disgusting," Payton said, coughing and holding her nose. "Her trifling ass has got to go."

"Maybe we can take these few bags here and drop them off somewhere?"

"I'm not putting those nasty bags in my car. How about we just put this shit outside."

"I don't think that's a good idea. People would probably walk away with the stuff and then you'd have more problems on your hands, with her trying to get more out of you than this junk is worth."

"The only thing remotely valuable in here is this old-ass computer and printer. I just want her and all her nasty shit out of here," she whined.

Tony placed his hands around her waist and guided her toward the door. "Why don't you call the number she gave you and leave her a message that we'll be back in a few hours? Then we could go find us some dinner."

The heel of Payton's shoe got stuck in a pile of dirty clothes and she almost lost her balance. "Damnit! I just want this shit to be over. I don't have time to keep traipsing out here with no results." She stormed out of the basement, her mind in overdrive. The spring property taxes were due in just a few weeks and she had promised herself last December that she'd paid her last tax bill on this house. The house needed to be sold.

When she made it to the end of the walkway, she reached for the latch to open the gate, but her hand impulsively went to the steel-gray metal box that was recessed into the side of the house. When she opened the box and pulled out the metal fuse that looked like a roll of quarters, a large grin spread across her face.

"I don't know why I didn't think of this sooner." She chuckled before she dropped the piece of metal into the palm of Tony's hand.

"What do you want me to do with this?"

"When I was growing up, this fuse was the cause of some powerless, hot, and restless summer nights. When it was really hot, which it always was in Pittsburg, this fuse would blow out and we'd lose all power to the house and have to wait until the morning for my granddaddy to go to the hardware store for a replacement," she said, sliding into the driver's side of her car. "I bet her ass will call me back now."

A few minutes later they arrived at New Mecca Restaurant in downtown Pittsburg. The familiar smell of refried beans and Mexican spices flooded Payton's senses. It brought back memories of her childhood and calmed her nerves. She opened the car door and placed one foot on the pavement.

Tony gestured toward the growing line outside. "Is this the only restaurant they have in Pittsburg?"

Payton grinned. "C'mon, boo, you're with me."

"So you got it like that?"

"Yeah, I got it like that." She closed the car door behind her.

They hurried past the crowd into the narrow restaurant. Lines of confusion marred Tony's broad forehead as he took in the bullhead mounted to the wall, with what looked to be a rolled joint hanging from its mouth and a bumper sticker plastered beneath it that read *No to drugs, yes to burritos.* Payton waited for the Latino man at the register to finish taking the payment from the customer in front of her. New Mecca didn't accept reservations, but before she'd picked up Tony from the Bart station she'd called ahead and Martine, a family friend, had promised to hold a table for her. A few moments later they were escorted to the next available booth.

"So tell me your secret."

"What secret are you referring to?" she asked, openly flirting with him across the table.

"Any secrets you want to share, but right now I'm most interested in how we were seated within five minutes when the sign upfront clearly states in bold letters they don't take reservations."

"Payton? *Mija?* Is that you?" said an attractive older Latina woman.

Grace Garcia, the waitress, had been working at New Mecca for decades and had served Payton and her grandparents for years when they came for their Friday night dining ritual. Grace's smooth brown skin was framed by salt-and-pepper strands pulled back away from her face.

Payton stood up and embraced the older woman in a brief yet familiar hug. "Grace, you look wonderful."

"You too, *mija*," Grace said, staring at Tony. "Is this your husband? You better not have gotten married and not invited your Mecca family to the wedding."

"No. This is my friend, Tony Barnes. Tony, this is Mrs. Grace."

"It's a pleasure to meet you, Mrs. Grace."

"The pleasure is mine," she said, shaking his hand. "So what brings you to our neck of the woods, *mija?*"

"I'm selling my grandparents' house and I had to take care of some business related to that."

"Well, I'm glad you stopped by for a visit. Now, what can I get you to drink?"

"I'll take my usual."

"I'll take a Heineken," Tony added.

"One Fanta Strawberry soda and a Heineken coming right up. I'll be back in a minute to take your food order."

Tony closed the menu in front of him.

"Fanta Strawberry?"

"Yeah, Fanta Strawberry. I've been drinking it since I was thirteen. I kinda grew up in this place," she noted again. "Have you decided what you'd like to eat?"

"What's good?"

"Everything. If you like Mexican, you can't go wrong here." For the first time it occurred to her that she didn't know if Tony liked Mexican food or not, and that she hadn't bothered to ask. "You do like Mexican, right?"

"Mexican is fine."

Grace returned with the restaurant's famous bean dip and their drinks. "Are you ready to order?"

"I'll have the Marcella special."

"What kind of meat?"

"Give me chicken for my taco and shredded beef for the burrito."

Grace turned to Tony. "What can I get for you?"

"I think I'll have the same."

They watched as Grace left their table and made her way to the window at the back of the restaurant, where she handed the order ticket to a woman in the kitchen.

When Payton looked back at him he was looking at her.

"What are you staring at?" She smiled at him across the table.

"You," he replied, taking a swig of his beer. "So, how are the renovations in the main area of the house coming along?"

"I spoke with the contractor earlier today and he's on schedule to finish the bathroom tile, the hardwood floors, and the painting by the end of next week. I'm going to call him tomorrow to see what he'll need to do in the basement once I get this woman out."

"Well, I'm no contractor, but the basement is finished. Once the trash and other stuff are removed, there won't be much to do down there besides applying a new coat of paint..." His voice trailed off when her cell phone rang.

She immediately accepted the call. "Payton Jones."

"Ma'am, this is Officer McGrady with the Pittsburg Police

Department. I've been called out to the property located at 625 West 12th Street in response to a complaint from your tenant."

"Tenant?" Payton spat, fighting to keep her voice controlled and casual. "Sir, I don't have a tenant at that property. No one lives at that address other than my uncle, who is currently incarcerated."

"Well, I have a Ms. Sonja Mitchell here with me and she claims that she has been living at the property and you turned the electricity off."

"As a matter of fact I did remove a fuse that powers electricity to the home. I don't have any type of agreement with Ms. Mitchell and she does not pay rent or utilities. I have communicated to her that she cannot live there and have made several arrangements with Ms. Mitchell to remove herself and her things from the property, but every time we schedule a time and I drive out to Pittsburg, she's not at the house."

"Ma'am, I understand your dilemma, but Ms. Mitchell has shown me mail she received at this address, she has belongings here, and a key, so by law she is a tenant."

Payton's mouth went dry as she processed what the officer had just shared with her. She spoke slowly, choosing her next words carefully. "No disrespect intended, Officer, but I don't have a contract or verbal agreement with Ms. Mitchell, so the tenant eviction laws do not apply. I need her out of my house today."

"It sounds like Ms. Mitchell is squatting on the property, but at this point there's nothing I can do. This is a civil matter and will have to be dealt with through civil court. You can go down to the Pittsburg courthouse on Monday to start the eviction proceedings. In the meantime, I need you to restore electricity to the home."

"You have got to be kidding," Payton answered, anger rushing into her voice.

"Sorry, ma'am, but I'm not. When can you return to the property with the fuse?"

"I'm in the middle of having dinner, but as soon as I'm done, I'll go back to the property and replace it."

"Would you please give us a call before you head back to the property so that I or another officer can be present?"

"Sure. I don't see that as a problem."

"Believe me, ma'am, the civil court system is the only way to handle this situation right now."

The officer was still talking, but Payton had already checked out of the conversation. The only thing on her mind at that moment was devising a plan to get that bitch out of her property. Pronto.

Chapter 20

Barbara Brown was finishing her Sunday evening stroll when she noticed a light blue Saturn stop alongside the Jameses' driveway. She'd stopped at the Unitarian Church to catch her breath and was hurrying home so she could watch *60 Minutes*. It was almost seven and she'd been out walking for almost an hour, but with daylight saving time there was still plenty of light for her to see clearly. The car looked like the same one she'd seen a few days earlier, parked across the street. She quickened her pace down the incline, careful not to lose her balance. As she moved closer, she caught a better glimpse of the female driver. The woman's dark sunglasses stood out against her pale yellow face—the kind of face that made men risk getting slapped to take a second look. The woman pressed a piece of paper against the steering wheel and began to write something. Then she folded the paper and sealed it in a large manila envelope with a swipe of her tongue.

Mrs. Brown continued to watch the woman, who looked like she was up to something.

The woman stepped out of the car, her hands pulling on the hem of her almost-nonexistent miniskirt, and moved toward the front gate where she lingered but never pressed the buzzer like a normal guest would. Instead, she creased the large envelope in half and attempted to stuff it into the mail slot that refused its size. The sound of Mrs. Brown's footsteps on the pavement pulled the woman out of her trance. She turned to find Mrs. Brown standing a few feet away, staring dead in her face.

The woman's body seemed to clench like a fist and went completely still. Nothing moved except her eyes, which darted behind her sunglasses, like a caged animal looking for an escape route.

"Can I help you, sugar?" Mrs. Brown questioned, eyeing the woman suspiciously and taking in all that could be seen up close. She was a thin girl with big breasts and long legs. Mrs. Brown lifted her expressive eyebrows, waiting for a response.

After a few moments of silence, the woman spoke. "No, thank you, ma'am, I was just leaving something for Dr.—"

"I can see that you leaving something, chile. The question is why you're putting something in this mailbox that has not made its way through the United States Postal Service. You know that's against the law, don't you?"

The envelope fell to the ground and Mrs. Brown caught a glimpse of who it was addressed to before the woman scrambled to pick it up.

"It looks like you are having trouble getting the package to fit in the mail slot. How about I do you a favor and give them the package?"

The woman raised her sunglasses and threw Mrs. Brown a dirty look. "Now why would I do that?" she asked, this time with more force and annoyance in her voice. "It's obvious you don't live at this address."

She turned her back to Mrs. Brown and attempted to push the envelope through the mail slot again.

"Didn't I see you over here a few days ago, leaving something?"

The woman ignored Mrs. Brown, shaking the envelope around to shift the contents.

"I can take that package for Donathan and make sure he gets it."

The woman turned around and stepped within inches of Mrs. Brown's face.

"Look, lady, I don't know who the hell you are, but what I am or am not leaving in this mailbox should be of no concern to you. You don't live at this address, so you need to mind your own fucking business."

Mrs. Brown leaned back in disbelief, responding as if the harsh words had slapped her across the face.

"Chile, have you lost your mind? You young people today don't have any manners. Didn't your mother teach you to respect your elders? All I asked was a simple question and it didn't warrant you disrespecting me."

"That sorry bitch that gave birth to me didn't teach me anything. Now if you don't leave me alone, I'm going to kick your old ass for summoning her into my memory today."

Mrs. Brown's face contorted and her mouth formed an oversize but silent O. She watched in astonishment as the young woman's persona changed. Her lips tightened and her features seemed to shift. She stooped down and passed the envelope through the wrought-iron gate and propped it up on the brick column where she'd left the last package. She turned to leave and purposely bumped Mrs. Brown, causing her to stumble backwards, but she quickly regained her footing.

"You disrespectful wench," she yelled after the woman, who was rushing toward her car. "Somebody needed to take a strap to your behind when you were growing up, or better yet wash your mouth out with soap. I've never heard such ugly words come from a woman's mouth."

Herbert Brown appeared in his doorway and yelled over to his wife. "Barbara, is everything okay over there? I can hear you carrying on all the way over here."

She didn't respond to her husband's question and her last words to the young woman had fallen on deaf ears as the Saturn sped away down Terrace Drive and made a sharp turn onto Moeser Lane. The woman's harsh words and body language were like the center pieces of a puzzle. They didn't make sense. She stirred the woman's behavior around in her mind, trying to make sense of the encounter before she reached inside the gate and retrieved the manila envelope. She would definitely give the package to Sydney.

With the package tucked underneath her arm, she hurried across the street and mounted the stairs that led to her front door. She was greeted by her curious husband.

"What you got there, Barbara?" Mr. Brown asked, his neatly trimmed salt-and-pepper mustache outlining his medium-sized lips. He stepped aside to allow her entrance into the house, but didn't close the door behind her.

"It's a package for the Jameses," Barbara said, hugging the envelope to her chest.

"Didn't I just see you reach behind their gate to pick up that package?" he said, eyeballing his wife and gathering the envelope for further inspection.

"I–I'm collecting the mail for them . . . they are out of town."

"You wouldn't be meddling in other folks' affairs, now would you?" Mr. Brown pointed in the direction of Donathan's car, which had just pulled up across the street. "I'ma go take this package to him right now."

"No, Herbert," she yelled, her voice escalating as she reached for the envelope. "I was going to give all the mail to Sydney when she gets back tomorrow."

"Now that doesn't make sense for us to hold their mail until tomorrow. Especially since the man just drove up. Do you have anything else for them?" He paused outside the front door.

"No," she replied, deflated.

"Well, you go on in and take a seat. I'll be right back to join you."

Mr. Brown waved the manila envelope and called out Donathan's name as he approached his vehicle. When he reached the car, he handed Donathan the package, his breathing labored.

"Barbara was under the impression that you and Sydney wouldn't be back until tomorrow and was holding this package for you, but I saw you drive up and rushed it right over."

⋆ ⋆ ⋆

Donathan took the envelope. "Thanks, Mr. Brown." He found the statement about him being out of town odd because Mrs. Brown had waved to him earlier when he'd left the house. "Did Mrs. Brown say who gave her the envelope?" he questioned, praying Austyn hadn't come into contact with his nosy neighbor.

"No, she didn't. I saw her talking to this young woman a few minutes ago, but if you need me to ask her—"

Donathan's stomach tightened. "That won't be necessary. You have a nice evening, Mr. Brown."

"You do the same, son."

Donathan entered the house and immediately disarmed the alarm system. His instincts told him what was inside the familiar envelope before he ripped it open to find more sexually explicit pictures of himself and Austyn. A note on vellum paper with scarlet-red writing fluttered through the air and caught his attention before it landed on the floor.

> *Donathan,*
> *Since your wife is out of town I was hoping we could get together tomorrow night and talk about our situation . . . meet me at Mimosa Champagne Lounge at 7:30 p.m. Until then, smooches.*
> *Austyn*

"Fuck!" The crumpled see-through paper disappeared into the confines of Donathan's hand. How the hell did Austyn know Sydney was out of town? And the last thing he needed her doing was continuing to stop by his home and interacting with Mrs. Brown. What if Sydney had gotten the packages instead of him? He walked to the panel to disarm the alarm, and the closed-circuit security monitor sparked his next move. He couldn't believe he hadn't thought of this sooner. He climbed the stairs two at a time to the second floor. He opened the door to the closet-sized room that housed the recorder for their home security system. He pressed

Rewind and then watched the monitor as the tape looped back-ward, summoning the light blue Saturn parked alongside his gate, a partial license plate number in clear view.

He released his cell phone from his belt clip and dialed Holsey. A partial plate was something.

Chapter 21

Joi drove down San Pablo Avenue, taking the long way home. She'd gone to Costco, then stopped by Good Vibrations to return the sex education videos she'd rented, but now she was furious. She'd just listened to a voice-mail message from Tyrese, who'd informed her that he wouldn't be leaving with them in the morning on their camping trip. What the hell was Tyrese doing? She shook her head at the thought of spending two whole days with two four-year-olds in the wilderness without him.

He'd said something about work, but she didn't believe him. Camping at East Park Reservoir was an annual thing for Joi's side of the family. Even her brother, Justin, who played professional basketball for the Sacramento Kings, made it a priority, and she didn't understand why Tyrese couldn't do the same. She sighed heavily. Who was she kidding? She did understand. Her husband was up to something and work had nothing to do with it.

She pulled into the driveway and carried one of the large Costco reusable bags inside the house. Tyrese met her at the door, removing the heavy bag from her grasp before bringing in the rest of the bags. When he placed the last bag on the counter, he found Joi hastily putting away the perishable items. They exchanged a long look before she moved around him and made a beeline for the other bags, distancing herself from him.

In silence, Joi put away the rest of the groceries, folded the reusable bags, and made sure everything was neat before she escaped into the family room and fell onto the couch. She picked up the remote control, and clicked on the television. Tyrese sat down close beside her and leaned in to kiss her on the neck.

"Stop it, Ty," she grumbled, pushing him away.

"Joi, stop playing. You know you like that," he said, flashing his knowing smile. When it came to sex, Joi never said no to her husband, but if he thought a little kiss on the neck would get him off the hook, he had another thing coming.

"Right now I don't," she shouted.

"I don't know why you're tripping. I'll be up there in less than forty-eight hours."

"Do you want to know why I'm tripping? Every year you do the same shit. You promised me last year you wouldn't do it again." Her eyes filled with tears. Out of control, she kept going. "How is it that my brother plays in the NBA and he can manage to leave with his family, but you can't?" The look on Ty's face made her want to take back her last words. His NBA career had been shattered by a knee injury and he was very sensitive about that.

He stared at her with a strange look in his eyes. "Listen to me," he said, his tone icy. "It's my job to take care of you and to put food on the table, and in order to do that I have to go to work."

"I have been listening to you," Joi interrupted. "I've listened to you nonstop this entire marriage." She stared at him accusingly. "You made a promise to me that we'd go on this camping trip together."

Tears began to fall down her cheeks and Tyrese pulled her into him.

"I know, baby, but please don't cry. You know I can't stand to see you cry," he said, kissing the wetness away.

Joi sat motionless, her movements noticeably measured. He continued his kisses and caressed her breasts. Her weak spot. Her nipples hardened and she felt the tingles of her arousal. She didn't want what he was doing to her to feel good, but it did. It wasn't so much the act as it was how she felt afterward. She felt empty and used. Before, making love to her husband used to be a happy experience, one that left her satisfied and content, but now after sex all she wanted to do was cry. She was tired of crying. All she wanted him to do was keep his promises and stop lying to her. She was depressed and confused, but she didn't want to give Tyrese any more reasons to stray. So she went along with his advances. She pushed him down on the sofa and straddled him. She could feel his erection growing against her bare leg.

"Where are the boys?"

"Taking a nap," he responded, kneading her nipples between his thumb and pointer finger. She closed her eyes and let her senses take over. He kissed her slowly and moved his hands up and down her back, finally finding their way under her skirt to her bare ass cheeks. She rolled her hips in a slow, sensual grind, her arousal heating up as she brushed herself against his manhood, pushing against the thin fabric that separated them.

She lifted his T-shirt over his head and kissed him hard, just like she had seen the girl do in the video. She kissed his chest and continued downward, lingering a while at the fine hairs that swirled around his navel. He leaned his head back and moaned. She undid his jeans and freed his manhood. She wrapped as much of her hand as she could around his girth and stroked him just the way he liked it. She felt liberated and in control.

"Let's go to the bedroom so we can make love."

"I want to ride your dick right here."

Tyrese tensed, locked eyes with her, but then relaxed into her strokes. Joi kissed him on the lips a few times then started her descend downward. She kissed his neck, his chest, his stomach and he moaned. He was very aroused, and she could feel his sense of control fly out the window. She leaned in to kiss his stomach again, except this time she brushed past his navel, her tongue stealing a swipe at his sex.

"That's it, baby," he said as she covered his pulsating member with her warm, wet mouth, and Joi moaned loudly, enjoying what her husband was finally letting her do. Suddenly, Tyrese's eyes popped open and he jumped up, sending his wife flying to the floor.

"What the hell are you doing?" He glared down at her in disgust. "I told you never to do that fucking shit. You put your mouth on my children."

Joi looked confused. All the videos she had been watching claimed men liked oral sex as long as you didn't use your teeth. She raked her fingers through her short, curly hair, still not comprehending what the big fucking deal was.

"I bet you don't mind when those other bitches suck your dick," she spat, feeling embarrassed and rejected.

"What the hell are you talking about? What bitches?" he said, his arms flailing about.

"I'm not stupid, Tyrese. I could tell you liked it and I'm smart enough to know if you're not getting it at home, you're getting it somewhere else," she said, searching his eyes for the truth.

"There you go, tripping," he said, helping her up off the floor. "Baby, you're beautiful and you're all I need." He kissed the insides of her palms, pleading with his eyes. "I understand you're trying to please me, but I just can't let my wife do that type of thing. You know I don't want anybody but you."

"I don't believe you. I know you let those whores suck your dick."

"Baby, I keep telling you, there are no other women."

Joi yanked her arm away. In her gut she felt this was just another one of his lies. "I need to finish packing." She stopped at the door, her voice wavering as she wiped her cheeks with the back of her hand.

"Have you seen Taylor's Game Boy?" she asked.

"Yeah, it's in the center console of my truck."

Once the garage door closed, Tyrese's head began to pound. Joi was right. He did love it when whores like Debbie sucked his dick, but the idea of spewing his seed down his wife's throat repulsed him. He massaged his temples, trying to stave off the intense headache that had been closing in on him all day. This day wasn't turning out the way he'd planned. Joi was again accusing him of seeing other women, and this was the second time in a matter of weeks that he'd refused a blow job from her. He had to admit her warm mouth felt damn good and it seemed like she knew what she was doing, which he had major concerns about. Any woman who put a dick in her mouth wasn't worthy to be the mother of his children. The thought of his boys swapping kisses with a woman who'd put her mouth on his pole was even more sickening. As far as he was concerned, dick sucking was off limits in the White household, and when things settled down, he'd make sure Joi understood that.

Joi stopped at the coat closet and took out the GPS device that had arrived on Saturday. She wanted the truth, but Tyrese was still lying to her face. She retrieved the Game Boy from the console and then strategically placed the tracking device under the driver's seat, as the instructions suggested.

With tears of frustration pooling in her eyes, she reentered the house, determined that the lies and deceit were about to come to an end.

CHAPTER 22

With traces of last week swirling through his mind, Donathan spent the entire afternoon preoccupied about his scheduled evening meeting with Austyn. His morning had flown by with abandon. This morning, in his role as the sex doctor, he'd taken audience questions and was alert enough to respond to them live on the radio show, but now he was alone in his office, mulling over his options. He read Sydney's itinerary and then reread the crinkled note from Austyn for what seemed like the hundredth time. There was no way he could be in two places at once, and not picking up Sydney from the airport would piss her off even more. He thought about picking her up, dropping her off at home, and running back out to meet Austyn, but he knew that would be cause for a lot of unanswerable questions, and he'd also run the risk of Austyn not being there if he was late. He picked up the phone and called Black Tie Limousine Service.

A few hours later Donathan parked his Mercedes along 24th Street in the artsy, uptown district of Oakland. With his game face on, he glanced down the street, measured the distance to the front door, and then trotted out into the darkness of the falling rain. He stepped inside the champagne lounge with the stride of a man at ease with himself. It was a weeknight and raining, but Mimosa was buzzing with after-work conversation. He removed his raincoat, brushed the droplets of water from his dark wool trousers, then searched the room for the woman who was determined to ruin his life. His mind wandered, as it always did when he was stressed, and he remembered he'd forgotten to call Sydney to make sure she'd received his message. But it was too late for that now.

He scanned the room and noticed the woman he was looking for perched at a small bistro-style table at the back of the lounge. As he passed numerous patrons, mostly women, a few of them clung to him, trying to persuade him to sit at their table, but he extracted himself with a polite shake of his head and a few kind words, reminding himself to stay focused. Before he could sit down, a waiter appeared out of nowhere.

"I'll have a small bottle of unopened Pellegrino," Donathan said before he sat down. He stared at Austyn. Her features were evenly distributed, perfect. She reminded him of a younger version of Sade. She matched his stare with a mocking smile, and he wanted to ask her what the fuck was so funny, but he desperately needed to keep his cool if he was going to get anywhere with her tonight.

The waiter returned within what seemed like seconds with the unopened bottle and scurried away to the next table.

"You look gorgeous tonight," he said, after pouring the sparkling water into his glass. "Have we met before?"

Austyn ran her tongue along her lower lip in the most provocative way. "Of course we've met before."

"No." He cut her off. "I'm talking about before the golf course. It's the oddest thing, but you remind me of someone," he added, noting her perfectly made-up eyes, wide and appealing. She looked much younger than he remembered, probably in her late twenties. She gave him a long, lingering look and leaned toward him, the cowl neck of her sweater dipped to expose her plentiful breasts.

"We all think we're original, but I can be whoever you need me to be," she purred and scooted her chair closer to his. "So when is your wife coming home?"

"I didn't come here to talk about my wife," he said, throwing off that bad-boy vibe women found irresistible. "How about we discuss why you wanted to meet me here tonight?"

"Well, I thought since you fucked me, the least you could do was take me out for a drink." Her eyes danced between him and the front door.

Donathan stared at her again. During the past week she had been relentless, showing up at his home and his office with those obscene pictures. If playing along with her insanity would get him what he needed, so be it.

"That's reason enough, don'tcha think?" she said, interrupting his thoughts.

He lowered his voice and turned on the bullshit charm that always worked so well for him. "Let's go back to your place. We can repeat what we did the other night, and then I'll at least have an active memory of what we did together."

"Why don't we go get a room? The Marriott is just up the street," she suggested. His phone rang, and she eyed him suspiciously. He removed it from his belt clip, did a quick scan of the screen, and then stabbed the unknown number into voice-mail oblivion. If it was urgent, they'd call his office and his service would call him back. He cleared his throat and continued.

"Hotels are so impersonal," he said, blowing a warm breath against her ear. She quivered from the heat, a chill running through her body. Then, without warning, Austyn faced him and covered his mouth with hers just in time for the flash from a camera. Donathan was startled. He got up, with the intention of spewing a tirade of insults, but thought better of it; he didn't want to attract any more attention to himself.

"Hey," he called out, taking huge strides to catch up with the man who was heading toward the front door. "What's up with the pictures?" he asked the man's retreating back.

The man stopped at the front door and faced Donathan. "Just a few promotional shots for the web site."

The photographer couldn't have been more than five-foot-eight. He was dressed for the rain and had water droplets resting in his medium-length afro. He looked like a black Columbo, if there was such a thing.

"I'm not interested in being on the Mimosa web site, and don't I need to sign a release for you to use my likeness?"

"In case you weren't aware, this is a public setting and releases aren't necessary. And who said anything about Mimosa's web site?" the photographer replied with a self-satisfied smile. "You have a nice evening, Dr. James."

Donathan stared at the photographer in disbelief as he passed through the glass entrance doors and imagined all the dreadful scenarios that could come from those pictures.

That conniving bitch, he thought. This was probably all her doing. A few days ago she was just another groupie. Now she was acting all smug, like she was running things. He backed away from the front door, turned on his heel, and rushed back to the table. When he got there she was gone. Donathan was livid. He couldn't believe he'd let her get away from him again. This new glitch changed everything. This was a fucking nightmare. He was sure the photographer was from a local rag and the picture of him and Austyn would be the lead story on the internet blogs come tomorrow. He didn't know which blog it was, but there was one thing he knew for sure: he had to come up with a new plan. His life was fucked up. Very fucked up. He grabbed his coat and was out of there.

Austyn sat in the driver's seat of the Saturn, soaked from head to toe. She had parked her car off Broadway, and in her hasty departure she'd left behind the three-dollar umbrella she'd purchased earlier. The rain had intensified and her breath was still coming in pants. The windshield wipers swayed back and forth as she pulled onto Telegraph and drove for a while before her car passed under the Highway 24 overpass. The car stopped in front of an obscure building, the words "Adult Bookstore" illuminated across the front. She parked, ran inside, and made her way toward the cashier. The lighting was bright, with the exception of the small hallway that led to a row of private booths. Shelves were lined with books and magazines, display tables strategically placed around the floor displaying sex toys, condoms, and lubricants. She reached into her purse, removed a ten-dollar bill, and handed it to the cashier.

After taking the roll of coins, she turned on her heel and bumped into a tall, slender man who'd been standing in the magazine section when she'd come in. They made eye contact and he held her gaze before she moved around him and headed in the direction of the dimly lit hallway. He grinned and followed at a distance, but Austyn could smell his closeness, a combination of a long day's work and stale beer. She yanked open the curtain to a vacant booth, sat down on a small stool, then pulled the black curtain closed behind her. After she inserted her first quarter into the machine, the shortened length of the black satin exposed the pair of muddied work boots that belonged to her admirer. Still standing, she pulled back the curtain and took in every inch of him. He wore jeans, a long-sleeved, orange T-shirt, and a fluorescent-green safety vest, the City of Oakland emblem printed on his left breast pocket. Without a word she stepped back, he stepped inside, and she closed the curtain behind him.

Chapter 23

Back at home, Joi used her nervous energy to clean the entire house, cook a romantic dinner, take a luxurious bath, and now she was agitated and tired of waiting for her husband to come home. Her brother and sister-in-law had agreed to take the boys up to the campsite with them, giving her and Tyrese some much needed adult time. The plan was for the two of them to drive up together the next day. She'd phoned him at his office at around twelve-thirty to let him know the change of plans, but his secretary had put her on hold for what seemed like an eternity and then returned to say that Mr. White wasn't available. It was now after seven o'clock and she still hadn't heard from him.

Joi stared at the coq au vin shriveling on the granite island. She was beginning to get antsy. Where was he? She hurried into the office, her mind conjuring up plenty of reasons why he hadn't made it home. And at the top of the list was because he was with one of his whores.

She typed in the GPS web site and her password on the laptop and paced back and forth as the screen slowly populated with a map. At first the entire state of California was on the screen, with one little red dot that represented Tyrese's truck. She clicked on the magnifying icon until the map zoomed in on the San Francisco Bay Area. The red light was now blinking, and she knew from the tutorial that the truck was moving. It looked like he was headed north on I-80. She blew out a ragged breath of guilt, chastising herself for overreacting, but her remorse faded as she watched the blinking dot take a right at the I-980 fork toward Walnut Creek and continue onto I-580 east, finally exiting at Harrison Street in Oakland. Where the hell was he headed?

She picked up her cell phone and punched in his number, but when the call went directly to his voice mail, she didn't bother to leave him a message. She continued to scrutinize the dot for a few minutes more before it stopped moving.

Joi waited a few moments before she clicked on the icon. It gave her an Oakland address on Martin Luther King Jr. Way. She wasn't familiar with the area and had no idea how long it would take her to drive from Hercules. She switched to the satellite view to get a better look. It showed a small, two-story building. Who was he visiting? She stared at the screen for what seemed like hours. Now what? Should she sit and wait for him to move or take matters into her own hands? She scribbled the address down on a piece of paper, then rushed up the stairs, into her walk-in closet. She pulled on an all-black sweat suit and a black baseball cap. Ten minutes later, she was on her way.

As Joi pulled onto Martin Luther King Jr. Way, she glanced at the clock on the dashboard. It had taken her thirty-five minutes door to door. She double-checked the address on the crumpled piece of paper and gazed around. She eyed two misfits loitering on the corner next to Eli's Mile High Club, a seedy-looking bar. She scanned the block for Tyrese's truck and tried to keep an open mind, but her instinct told her a woman was the only type of business her husband could have in this part of Oakland.

She parked her SUV two blocks away and hurried back toward the sound of B. B. King's "The Thrill Is Gone." The stench of too many folks living on a small land mass seeped from the apartment buildings and made it hard for her to remain focused.

What was she going to do? She didn't have a plan and there were so many unknowns to consider. She felt like a naïve young girl instead of the grown married woman she was. She'd tried to be a good wife and worked hard at doing all the things she was sure she needed to do to keep her husband happy. She cooked, cleaned, took care of the children, and paid extra attention to her appearance. And she willingly gave him sex whenever he initiated the act. She cringed now at the memory of his face twisted in disgust when he'd refused to partake in oral sex with her the day before. From the videos she'd watched, his response just didn't make sense. She'd rented and rerented the educational videos until she felt comfortable that she'd perfected the art of the blow job and was eager to test her new skills on her husband. When she had coffee with the moms from the boys' playgroup she always listened carefully when the conversations drifted to sex. At first she'd been embarrassed about discussing the topic but later had realized she didn't have to share with the other mothers that she'd never given her husband head. She'd learned to smile, nod, and give um-hums at the right intervals and they were none the wiser. It was because of them that she'd gotten up the nerve to venture into Good Vibrations in the first place.

She was so caught up in these thoughts that she almost walked on by the truck. She brushed her hand over the lukewarm hood and felt her pulse kick into high gear. She looked toward the entrance of the apartment complex, but she had no idea who she was looking for. Maybe if she pressed a few names someone would buzz her in. When she heard her husband's familiar voice from the other side of the gate she almost fainted. With her breath caught in her chest, she moved into the darkness and squatted down behind a parked car. What the hell was she going to do now? Her first instinct was to confront the lying, cheating son of a bitch, but the voice of Chase Morgan stilled her: Catching Tyrese exiting an apartment complex with a woman wasn't enough to secure the future of her children. At this point it would be his word against hers; like Mr. Morgan had said, she needed concrete proof.

Joi's eyes followed the two shadows as they exited the secured gate and strolled past her hiding place. They walked in the direction of the bar and once they turned the corner, Joi waited a beat, then followed.

Inside Eli's, Joi made a beeline for an empty booth in the back of the dark club that gave her a perfect view and a perfect hideaway. She hadn't seen him leave the house, but even with his back to her, she could tell Tyrese was dressed to kill in his charcoal-gray Armani suit, his sky-blue shirt peeking over his collar. She'd bet money he had on the charcoal tie with the light blue pinstripes, a combination that accentuated his piercing gray eyes—impeccable, if she had to say so herself. The girl brought to mind a two-dollar whore you could pick up off West MacArthur Boulevard back in the day, and she couldn't seem to keep her hands off Tyrese. Her fuchsia wrap dress was too tight, revealing an unsightly panty line that cut into her skin. The girl sat perched on his lap, cooing in his face and caressing his bald head; her shoulder-length weave was matted and begging for a comb.

Joi's face felt flushed and she cast her eyes downward before drinking a gulp of her water. He was definitely fucking her, she mused, fuming at the thought. Maybe it had been a mistake to follow them; she didn't know if she could stomach this. She'd only been there a few minutes and had already grown tired of the inappropriate touching. She was ready to pounce on that bitch like a cat. When the woman excused herself and headed in the direction of the ladies' room, Joi followed to get a closer look. She eased into the restroom and ducked into the adjacent stall, where she could hear the woman talking on the phone.

"Girl, I got his trick ass over here at Eli's right now and he's about to give me twelve hundred dollars for that Louis Vuitton bag I put on hold at the Union Square store today."

The volume of the phone was so loud that Joi could hear the person on the other end squawk her response. "Bitch, his ass isn't going to give you twelve hundred dollars."

"Like hell he ain't," the fuchsia girl snapped. The jingles from her bangle bracelets mingled with the sound of the flushing toilet.

"My mama didn't raise no fool, and if he knows what's good

for him and that good-paying job of his, he better give me my money tonight," she said. "Besides, they don't call me the head doctor for nothing." She giggled.

Joi's ears began to ring. She couldn't believe what she was hearing. Did that whore just say Tyrese was going to give her twelve hundred dollars? If Joi asked Tyrese for that much money, she would have to go through a full-press interrogation as to why she needed that much cash and sign her full name in blood, yet he was willing to freely hand over that much money to some skanky, classless bitch. This was un-fucking-believable.

She swallowed back a rush of bile and silently peeked through the crack in the door, watching the fuchsia girl as she stumbled out of the stall with the cell phone still perched between her shoulder and her ear. She adjusted her breasts and gave herself a once-over before exiting the restroom.

Joi took slow breaths in and out to control her emotions. She didn't know how or when, but his ass was going to pay for this, she thought, as she perused a framed plaque that paid tribute to Eli Thornton, the original owner of the club. According to the plaque, he had been shot to death by his jealous mistress, a blues singer. Joi studied the seventies photograph immortalizing Eli and wondered what he'd done to make his mistress take his life, but his charismatic smile told her all she needed to know: he had been a cheating bastard, just like Tyrese.

She eased back into her booth just in time to see a gangly man with skin the texture of dried leather hand Tyrese a business card and head in her direction, passing the fuchsia girl as she returned to Tyrese's table. Joi studied him closely as he entered the narrow hallway and bumped into a woman exiting the ladies' room.

"Excuse me," he croaked.

Joi's eyes opened wide with recognition. It was Curtis Holsey, the private investigator she'd hired a few days earlier. Oh my God! She didn't want him to see her. She glanced toward her husband again and saw the fuchsia girl coyly bent over at the waist with the fabric of her dress riding up so high it exposed the cheeks of her bare ass, backed up right in Tyrese's face. Joi turned away and tried not to think about how much she wanted to slap the shit out of her husband, whose attention hadn't wavered from what the girl was showing him. Fuchsia girl swayed her body to the upbeat blues tempo and pulled a reluctant Tyrese to the tiny dance floor.

Joi had seen enough. This was the moment to make her exit. She adjusted the bib of her cap to hide her face. As she hurried down the hallway, she grabbed a dirty steak knife off the busboy's station next to the kitchen. She slipped it into her tote bag as she hurried out the back door.

Outside the club, she moved hastily up the street. Aside from her, the same two misfits she'd seen earlier were the only ones standing across the street.

They called to her. "Can I take you home tonight, Mami?"

Joi ignored them as she made her way to her husband's truck. She removed the steak knife from her bag and stooped low. Like a stealth plane, she hovered around the truck, jabbed all four of his tires, and left behind the consistent sound of synchronized hissing in her wake.

She returned the knife to her tote and glided the few remaining blocks to her car.

"Damn, that felt good," she said out loud as she eased into the driver's seat of her SUV. "Now let's see how his smart ass gets out of this one."

Thirty minutes later Joi was back in the confines of her community, where she stopped at the local Safeway. With a single ear bud pressed in her ear, she made her way to the beverage aisle.

"How is it going up there?" Joi asked her sister-in-law, Gina. She could hear her boys in the background, asking to speak to her and their father.

"Everything is fine, sis. The kids just finished roasting marshmallows and we're about to put them down for the night. I promised they could call you and Tyrese so you could tell them good night."

Joi paused. How was she going to explain this mess to her children? They were too young to understand and her heart ached for them. She bit her bottom lip, worrying about her husband's way-wardness. They were boys and they needed their daddy. It became crystal clear that telling her sons their father wasn't going to say good night to them was something she had no plans on getting used to doing. She grabbed a six-pack of ginger ale, Tyrese's favorite, then made her way to the pharmacy to get what she needed.

"Go ahead and put them on speakerphone, Gina. I'm out at the store, so I'll just send them off to Mr. Sandman myself."

Joi stood in the checkout line with the ginger ale in one hand and a tiny brown bottle of syrup of ipecac in the other. She kissed her boys good night through the phone and reassured them that she and Tyrese would see them in a few days. She had no plans to raise her children in a single-parent home in the middle of the ghetto. She would have to use what she had to keep what belonged to her.

Chapter 24

The Superior Courthouse was located on Civic Drive in Pittsburg. The empty, well-manicured lots that in recent years had replaced the row of blighted properties once lining Railroad Avenue was the first thing Payton saw when she entered the city, jarring memories from her childhood.

One of the lots used to be home to JD's Barber Shop, a Pittsburg institution where Payton's grandfather, father, and uncles all went to get their hair cut and the wisdom of barbershop conversation. That was a pleasant memory. Mostly what Payton remembered about growing up in Pittsburg was tragedy and disappointment. Her father, Sonny, had been murdered over a dice game gone wrong in the back of Mac Lewis's record shop when she was ten. One day her mother, Lois, who coped with the death of her husband by self-medicating, failed to pick up Payton from the Brenden movie theater after she'd dropped her off to hang out with her friends. Payton was thirteen years old at the time; she knew right away that her mother was never coming back for her, though her grandmother wasn't convinced. Even after a year, when her mother still hadn't shown up, her grandmother clung tightly to her idea. Payton was sure her grandmother had gone to her grave not accepting that Lois had abandoned her.

She entered the courthouse, passed through the metal detectors, and walked directly to the room that handled civil matters. She had lived in Pittsburg most of her life, but this was her first time here. She stood in line, studying the notepad with all the legal advice she had obtained regarding this matter. She had spoken to several attorneys over the past few days and they'd all said the same thing: She had to evict Sonja Mitchell as if she were a tenant.

Payton approached the available window, and removed the thirty-day notice she'd obtained from the internet and the additional copies she'd been instructed to bring along for filing. She handed the clerk her paperwork and he scanned them for completion.

"That will be three hundred dollars, ma'am," he said, readying the filing stamp.

She fished her wallet from her handbag and extracted three crisp hundred-dollar bills, handed them to the clerk, and made a mental note to add this to the estate expenses. The clerk stamped the thirty-day notice form and four copies with a case number, making them official.

"You have to have someone over the age of eighteen serve these papers to the tenant," he said. "Then the server has to sign here, saying they did so, and return the form to the court. That way if the tenant fails to move and you have to file an eviction lawsuit, all the paperwork will be in order."

"I've been having a problem with the tenant not being home when I go to the property."

"All the person who's serving this notice has to do is post this on the front door of the property in a visible place and then mail one of these copies to the tenant at the address. Then they have to check the appropriate boxes and mail or bring the signed copy back to us for the record."

Twenty minutes later Payton emerged from the courthouse, knowing there was no way she could wait thirty-plus days to evict Sonja the legal way. Instead, she imagined offering her five hundred dollars in cash in small bills. If need be, she would go up to a thousand. There was no way a crackhead was going to turn down that much cash. Then Payton would pack up all Sonja's belongings and take her to a notary to sign a statement that she had moved out of the property and relinquished all her tenant rights. Once she signed, Payton would give her the cash and take her wherever she wanted to go and be done with it.

As she approached her car, she could see a tall, slender figure leaning leisurely against her car, holding a bicycle. As she moved closer she could see the figure was her uncle, Sheldon.

"What you doing here, Niecy?"

He was dressed in a red sweatshirt three sizes too large, heavily soiled jeans, and a pair of Chuck Taylor All Stars without socks. He attempted to hug her, but the disgusting odor that emanated from his body placed a sneer on her face that told him to back off.

"You ain't down here snitching on me, are you?" he asked, flapping his arms up and down, fanning his funk.

"Sheldon, you need to take a bath."

"If you give me fifty dollars I could go get a room at the Mar-Ray Motel, get cleaned up and get me something to eat."

Payton looked her uncle up and down, knowing if she gave him fifty dollars the last thing he was going to do was get a room or food.

"Uncle Sheldon, have you given any more thought to my offer? If you go to rehab, I'll pay your rent for six months after you get out, giving you some time to get yourself together. And I won't take this money out of your share from the sale of the house."

"Girl, I don' told you that I'm not going to no damn rehab."

"I bet my granddaddy Jones is turning over in his grave, seeing two of his sons acting like homeless—"

"If you hadn't kicked me out of my house, I wouldn't be homeless," he said, closing the distance between them.

Payton coughed. "If I hadn't kicked you out, the city would have red-tagged it and kicked you out for me. Then we all would have been screwed. The place was a mess. All that trash and exposed wiring—I had to pay the contractors a lot of money to get that house back to a sellable condition. The best thing for everybody is to sell it, take the money, and run."

"You don't have a right to sell a damn thing. That's my mama and daddy's house," he said, slurring his words. Sheldon was so drunk, his eyes were bloodshot and spittle was flying everywhere.

Payton fired a nasty look in his direction. "Right? In case you forgot, you lost your right when you started using dope, which is why Granddaddy gave me the right in the first place. While you chose to stand on the corner and get high, I was the one who has been paying the taxes, insurance, and maintenance for years, so that alone has earned me the right to do just what I'm going to do—and that's sell it."

She unlocked the car door with a chirp and dashed around him. "Grown-ass men thinking they can live somewhere for free," she mumbled. As far as she was concerned, this little impromptu conversation was over. It was one thing to have a conversation with rational people, but she had learned over the years that the entitlement her uncle Sheldon felt clouded his judgment, and she'd be damned if she was going to stand there and continue a conversation with a fifty-year-old man on a bicycle.

He yelled at her as she started her engine and backed out of the parking space.

"You need to stop acting like you all high and mighty. I told yo' mama when she started coming back around here, looking for you, that your uppity ass wouldn't give her the time of day. You ain't better than me. Whether you know it or not, we cut from the same fucking cloth."

Payton came to a head-jerking halt; her uncle's words involuntarily willed her leg to press on the brakes. She put the car in Park. Did she just hear him say her mother had been looking for her? She leaped out of the car and watched her uncle look back at her before he crossed Civic Drive.

"Wait! What did you just say?"

"Make sure you come to that corner and find me when you got my damn money," he said. "I'll wait then." His voice faded over his retreating back as he peddled vigorously and disappeared out of her sight into the city park.

Payton's heart began to beat erratically. It had been twenty-five years since she'd seen her mother. She could pass her on the street and not even know who she was. *Why fucking now?* Payton cringed. The bitch wanted something, and Payton wanted no part of that. "Fuck! Fuck! Fuck!" she yelled, her eyes drifting upward.

"I cannot deal with this shit right now," she screamed as she got back in her car, started the engine, and headed toward 10th Street.

With her thoughts still stuck on her uncle Sheldon's comments about her mother, Payton sat outside the Golden Star Market, her cell phone glued to the right side of her face. She made a call to Officer McGrady to let him know she was on her way to serve Sonja with eviction papers, and then she listened to her voice-mail messages. The first was from the real estate investor who had phoned to let her know he was prepared to close on the property next week and the second was from the contractor, who wanted to start the final work on the basement on Saturday. She sighed heavily. She desperately needed her plan to work. Otherwise this deal would fall through, and with the real estate market changing by the day, she wasn't sure if she'd be able to find another buyer willing to pay this price. The house should bring a lot more, but considering the condition it was in and for her peace of mind, the price was fair enough.

Minutes later Manny Perez, whose father owned the Golden Star Market, followed Payton around the corner to the house. With young Manny at her side, she knocked on the side door that led to the basement. After several minutes of waiting without an answer, she instructed Manny where to tape the notice and had him complete the paperwork. She sealed it and the additional envelopes she had already addressed. Then she gave Manny twenty-five dollars, and he left her standing on the narrow side walkway.

As soon as Manny disappeared, Payton slipped the key into the security screen and entered the basement, making sure to hold her breath. She half-expected the smells of rotting food and dirty clothes to jump out at her, but they didn't. The trash bags filled with clothes and the old fast-food containers were gone; the basement was empty except for the computer and printer and, upon closer inspection, a small stack of blank computer checks with her uncle's name, Donald Jones, Sr., imprinted on them.

"Hello," a voice called from the alleyway. Payton walked over to the wrought-iron gate.

"Can I help you?" she asked, appraising the man from head to toe as she took in the dark sunglasses, his dark blue uniform, and the handgun that rested neatly in its holster on his right side.

"Ms. Jones?"

"Yes," she said, extending the tip of her well-manicured hand for a formal shake.

"I'm Officer McGrady," he responded, "but please call me Mac. I got your message that you were coming down here to serve Ms. Mitchell and I thought I'd come by to—"

"Look, I'm doing everything by the book, even though I find it ludicrous to have to evict someone I've never had a contract with. I had Manuel Perez serve the papers and he just left."

"Slow down, Ms. Jones," Officer McGrady instructed, interrupting her tirade. She turned on her heels, headed toward the printer, then retrieved the small stack of checks.

"Look at this." She shoved the checks into the officer's hand and watched closely as he scanned the documents.

"Why are you giving these to me?"

"Because my *tenant* is up to no good. My uncle has been in jail for three weeks and his lifestyle doesn't afford him the luxury of a checking account. Sonja Mitchell knows he's coming into some money once we sell this house and I know these checks are fake."

Officer McGrady studied the checks further. They looked valid, but these days most fraudulent checks did.

"My uncle Donald doesn't have a valid California driver's license or identification card, so he couldn't legally open a checking account."

"As I was saying before, the reason I came down here was to apologize for not doing a warrant check on Ms. Mitchell last week. Turns out she was arrested yesterday for passing bad checks at Walmart. After we picked her up, it was later discovered there was a warrant for her arrest for a probation violation."

"How long is she going to be in jail?"

"Ms. Mitchell will be in jail for at least ninety days." He removed his sunglasses and looked around the room. "Have you touched anything else in here besides these checks?"

She looked at him strangely. "No. I hadn't been inside long before you arrived. Why?"

"Can you excuse me for a few minutes while I contact the detectives working on her case to see if they want to get a warrant for these checks, the computer, and the printer?" He walked away, speaking into the radio attached to his left shoulder.

Payton wanted to scream, but she didn't say a word. Sonja Mitchell would be tucked away for at least ninety days and that was more time than she needed to be rid of her squatting ass.

Payton's troubles with the house were nearly over. She moved to the corner and dialed a number that had become familiar to her over the past few months, eager to share her news. When the call went directly to Tony's voice mail her mood shifted. That feeling of disappointment was exactly why she didn't do relationships. She hadn't heard from Tony in four days, even though she'd left him several messages. She knew his mother was dying, but the least he could do was call her back. She sighed, chastising herself for forgetting the fact that she couldn't depend on anyone but herself. She left a message, her voice cold and firm.

"Y'know, I thought we were better than this, but obviously I was wrong. I've left three messages for you with no return call, so I guess this means you only call me when you need something. Don't bother calling me back; just lose my fucking number." She hung up the phone.

The tears appeared out of nowhere, threatening to spill from her eyes. But she fought hard to retract them, refused to let them fall. She'd made it this far without needing anybody and she sure as hell didn't need him.

Chapter 25

Sydney guided a medical student through a spinal tap on a six-week-old baby who had been born prematurely. She prayed the infant was negative for the respiratory syncytial virus that plagued so many babies this time of year, but it would take a few days before they knew for sure. Miles poked his head into the exam room, breaking her concentration.

"We've got work coming in," he announced, looking from the medical student to Sydney.

"What is it?" she asked, never taking her eyes off the medical student.

"There are two—a nine-month-old who fell from a four-story window and a two-year-old hit in the stomach by random gunfire. They're both about five minutes out," he answered, backing out of the doorway.

Sydney watched closely as the student removed the needle from the baby's lumbar vertebrae, careful not to make any sudden moves, as instructed. Once the needle was fully removed, the student backed away, and Sydney affixed a small bandage to the baby's skin. The student then handed her the small circular tube of fluid, which she held up to the light for inspection.

"What do you think?" the student asked.

"It should be clear, like water. Cloudy fluid like this might indicate meningitis," Sydney said, lifting the lethargic infant.

"Go ahead and start an IV on the baby so as soon as they get her settled upstairs, we can start the antibiotics. But first bring her family back so I can give them an update."

A young woman with an electric-blue braided ponytail entered the room. Her visible fear and worry manifested itself in the rings of moisture under both armpits of her dingy T-shirt. Tamara Freeman couldn't have been more than seventeen.

"Tamara, I'm Dr. James," she said, handing the young girl the baby. "We just completed the spinal tap on Leeshelle. Although it will take twenty-four hours to get the results back from the test for meningitis, the spinal fluid was a little cloudy, so as a precaution we're going to go ahead and start antibiotics immediately."

"What about the RSV test?" the young woman questioned, holding the baby close to her chest.

"We ran the respiratory syncytial virus test also; unfortunately, that test won't come back for a few days."

"I don't want my baby to die," the girl pleaded, her face riddled with fear.

"Sweetie, you did the right thing by bringing her in to the emergency room. I'm going to admit her and we're going to do everything in our power to get her back healthy and thriving. Okay?"

The young woman hesitated. "Okay. But will I be able to stay with her?"

"It won't be the most comfortable stay, but there are rocking chairs in the intensive care nursery."

The girl smiled and placed her free hand on Sydney's arm. "Thank you, Dr. James."

"You're welcome, Tamara. The other doctor will be in soon to start an IV on the baby and get her settled upstairs. I'll check back on the two of you a little later."

Sydney left the room, heading toward the emergency bay. She was impressed by the young mother and confident the baby would be okay. Tamara Freeman had blue hair, but she was articulate and asked all the right questions.

Through the luck of the draw, Sydney had inherited the gunshot victim. They'd taken the child to surgery and now, three hours later, he was stable, but all she could think about was whether he'd regain full use of his legs. The child had been hit by a stray bullet as he lay sleeping in bed with his parents. The senseless gun violence in Oakland had to end.

Sydney sat down at the nurses' station, further reflecting on her day. It was almost over, but the last fifteen minutes couldn't come soon enough. She'd already given reports and finished her charting. To pass the time, she surfed the internet, eventually finding her way to the celebrity gossip sites she enjoyed. She scrolled her way through bossip.com, theybf.com, and finally made her way to karma.com, a local Bay Area site.

The headline jumped out at her: *The Sex Doctor Is Making House Calls.*

Underneath the headline was a picture of Donathan, clearly upset and reaching for the camera. Sydney clicked on the "view pictures/read more" link and scanned the article. The headline was brutal enough, but the rest of the photos were worse. Her husband was in a serious lip lock with an unknown woman and, according to the web site, the photos had been taken just the night before. The site even had posted a photo of Donathan and Sydney for confirmation that he was a married man.

Sydney could feel fury building inside her like a volcano about to blow. That bastard! He had to know this shit was on the internet and his cowardly ass hadn't even tried to warn her. The web site she cruised for entertainment now had everyone laughing today— at her expense.

"I see you like to read karma.com, too," Miles said, craning his neck to peek over her shoulder. "Which lunatic is on blast today?" he asked before he recognized the man on the screen. He had never met Donathan in person but had seen his likeness on the numerous billboards plastered around the city.

"Is that who I think it is?" he asked to Sydney's stiffening back. She grabbed the computer power cord and yanked it from the electrical outlet, causing the screen to go black. She spun around and stared at Miles, saying nothing, but the fire in her eyes made it clear she was ready to burn the place down.

Without a word, she headed down the corridor to the doctors' quarters. When the door failed to close behind her, she realized Miles was on her heels.

"Are you okay?" he asked, his frame crowding the doorway.

Sydney removed her Crocs and reached for the sneakers perched at the bottom of her locker. She sat on the bench, closed her eyes, and took a deep breath. But the horrendous picture rested on the inside of her eyelids.

Finally, she responded, "I will be," but she refused to look at him. Not only had Miles seen everything, but she was sure everyone else had, too, and she was mortified. How was she going to show her face around here again?

She removed her lab coat, tossed it in the soiled linen receptacle in the corner, and sat back down on the bench to put on her shoes. Miles sat down beside her.

"I'm a good listener. How about we go grab a bite to eat?"

Sydney appreciated the gesture, but she wanted to be alone. The last thing she wanted to do was be seen in public. She wished she could just disappear.

"Excuse me," she said, reaching under his leg to pick up her other sneaker.

"If you want to talk about this, you know I'm here for you, right?"

He watched in silence as she tied one lace and then the other.

She finally looked at him, her eyes burning with anger, pleading for him to back off. "Miles, I know you mean well, but now is not a good time." Sydney stood up to leave. "Now, if you'll excuse me, I need to get the hell out of here."

The drive to El Cerrito was quick. When Sydney arrived home, Donathan's Mercedes was parked in the driveway. She pulled in behind him and entered the house, dropping her keys on the foyer table. She noticed he was in his office but didn't say a word; instead, she climbed the stairs to the master suite, two at a time. She entered her walk-in closet, removed her overnight bag from the shelf, and began methodically selecting pieces. Donathan appeared in the doorway.

"Is everything okay?" he said as he leaned against the door-jamb and folded his arms tightly across his chest.

Sydney ignored him, continuing to stuff items into her bag.

"What are you doing?"

"I'm getting the fuck out of here."

He looked genuinely surprised.

"What is this about, Sydney?" he said, closing the space be-tween them.

She pulled away from him, opened her underwear drawer, and grabbed a handful of her personals.

"Baby, whatever it is, we can fix this," he said.

"Fix this!" Her voice escalated. "You should have thought about that before you humiliated me by putting your mouth on some bitch who was not me. And then being stupid enough to let your fucking picture get taken and plastered all over karma.com."

Donathan stood frozen. Sydney found herself staring at the stranger in front of her who had promised to love, honor, and cherish her before God. She wasn't feeling honored at the mo-ment.

"Say something damn it!"

"Baby, I know you're upset, but it's not what you think," he pleaded, again reaching for her arm. She yanked it away.

"You have no idea what I think," she said and jabbed her index finger into the center of his forehead. "I don't know what the hell it is, but I sure know what the fuck it looks like."

She moved around him to the vanity area to collect some toi-letries.

"C'mon, Syd, you gotta listen to me. Can we talk about this? Baby, please, you have to listen to me."

"Give me one good reason." She stepped out of her scrubs and shimmied into a pair of jeans and a tank top. There was a pause, as if Donathan hadn't expected that she would do anything other than listen.

"Because you need to have all the facts before you walk out the door."

Facts or no facts, there was no way she was going to sleep under the same roof with him tonight. She needed space to clear her head and figure out how she would ever be able to walk into the hospital with her head held high after this mess.

She looked at his reflection in the vanity as she brushed her hair into a ponytail. "Talk."

He shifted his weight, not into a fighting stance, but to show a man who'd had all the wind knocked from his sails. She turned to face him, waving her brush in his face.

"I'm a thirty-eight-year-old professional woman who loves her husband and was under the impression the feeling was reciprocated and this is how you repay me? You could have at least given me the common courtesy to do that shit behind closed doors."

Donathan simply stared at her.

"Do you love this woman?"

"Love her? You've got to be fucking kidding me. This woman is ruining my life."

"Ruining *your* life? How do you expect me to go to work? All these years I've put up with people talking behind my back because of you, walking into rooms and feeling like everyone knows the secret except me because of you. Well, 'Sex Doctor' James, you are on notice that this is the first and last time I will let you do this to me." She slipped into her flipflops, moved past him, grabbed the overnight bag, and headed for the door.

Donathan's first instinct was to go after her, but he knew Sydney well. The last thing he should do was try to stop her. What he needed to do was get to the bottom of this, to show her that for once he hadn't done anything wrong.

When he heard the front door slam shut he hurried back to his office. He typed in karma.com on his computer and viewed the photos. The first was a harsh black-and-white of him clearly upset about having his picture taken and the last was a full-color image worth a thousand words. He and Austyn were in what appeared to be a sensuous lip lock. They looked like lovers.

"God damn it," he screamed, knocking the glass vase off his desk. He was a fucking idiot! This was another setup and he'd walked right into it again. In his mind, he'd gone to Mimosa to shift the power dynamic, but it was clear from these pictures that Austyn was still the one with the upper hand.

He understood why Sydney was so upset, but there was nothing he could do about it. This wasn't his first tabloid storm, and in his line of work it definitely wouldn't be his last. By next week he'd be old news. These pictures were bad, but not as damaging as the ones Austyn had taken of them together at the Marriott. If she circulated those pictures . . . all hell would break loose.

Chapter 26

Payton sat on her sofa, binge watching DVR episodes of her latest shows, a Friday-night ritual when she didn't have a date. But tonight the recorded line up failed miserably at holding her attention. Flashes of her mother dropping her off at the movie theater, the memories she had long ago suppressed, had haunted her since her uncle had mentioned that her mother was looking for her. She hated the vulnerability of the thirteen-year-old girl she was back then, who wanted nothing more than for her mother to come back for her. But twenty-five years later wasn't exactly what that girl—or Payton—had in mind. Competing with those thoughts was the fact that she still hadn't heard from Tony. She'd hurried home from her Zumba workout at Fitbody, sporadically peering at her iPhone the whole drive home to see if she had missed a call or text from him. How had she let herself get caught up enough to care? She told him never to call again, but he had to know she didn't mean that.

She muted the television and picked up her cell phone again. She scrolled through her contacts, located his name, and sent him a text message containing all capital letters:

FUCK YOU!

No sooner had she placed the device back down on the table than it vibrated, as if responding to her harsh words. She picked it up and grinned. It was a text message from David, a friend with benefits—just what she needed right now.

Hey

Payton fell back onto the couch, contemplating the three little letters, which in most cases were harmless; but if she responded, she would end up facedown, ass up, with another woman's husband stroking her into submission.

She'd tried PerfectChemistry.com; those boring fucks weren't worth her time. Tony had been filling her sexual void, but now he'd vanished off the face of the earth. She ruminated over what she'd do next. The thought of a no-strings-attached tryst aroused her. No cuddling, talking, invasion of her personal space—just a good fuck and then get the fuck out. And his head game was on point. Her fingers involuntarily began typing.

Hey

What are you wearing?

Nothing . . . I'm painting my toes fire-engine red.

Sounds pretty. Can I suck them for you when you're done?

Depends.

On what?

What else u r going to suck on after ur done with my toes?

Baby, you know me. I'll suck your toes and a few other things.

Tell me more about those other things?

I follow directions really well. Send me a pic of what you want me to suck.

Payton rolled the strap of her tank top down her left arm and exposed one breast. She snapped a picture of her nipple, briefly inspected the image, then pressed Send and waited.

Ur nipple is hard . . . looks like u need some attention.

I'm getting wet just thinking about ur type of attention.

Her house phone rang. She ignored it.

Can I come over?

She typed in **Yes**, but before she could hit Send, Sydney's voice sounded through the speakers of her message recorder.

"Payton, pick up," she said, her voice sounding agitated. "I'm coming over. I need to talk." Before Payton could react, she heard a dial tone.

"Damn," Payton said, sinking back into the couch and backspacing three spaces. She erased the word and began to type.

R u going to b out 4 a while.

I hope not.

I need a rain check.

A rain check? C'mon, baby, let me put us both out of our misery.

Nothin I'd love to do more right now...but can't tonight.

Can I take you to dinner tomorrow?

Ooo you want to play outside? Where's the head bitch in charge?

How about Picán...say 8?

I'll call u in the a.m.

Without waiting for his response, she put her phone on the charger and headed to the kitchen to refresh her drink. She didn't know what Donathan had done, but he had cost her a much-needed orgasm. And from the sound of Sydney's voice, Payton knew another drink was in order to calm her nerves before the storm.

Two more Hennessey brambles and thirty minutes later, Payton was sitting next to Sydney, consoling her.

"What happened, Syd?" she asked, feeling relaxed from her drinks but not so much so that she had forgotten about her mother or Tony. She was trying to feign interest in what was really going on with Sydney and Donathan when the fact of the matter was, she had way too much on her own plate to muster up genuine concern for her friend.

"I just don't understand why he would do this to me," Sydney said, rubbing her temples like she was trying to ward off a headache.

"Do what?" Payton questioned, and Sydney scowled at the response. "Look, Syd, you know I'm challenged in the listening department. You need to come out with it so we can get to the bottom of why you're sitting on my couch talking but not really saying anything."

Sydney leaned forward, avoiding eye contact with Payton. She took a deep breath and exhaled her next words.

"Donathan is cheating on me."

"Girl, is that it?" Payton responded, sucking her teeth and rolling her eyes upward. "All men cheat on their wives. . . . Here you had me thinking somebody was dead or about to die."

"Payton, this is my marriage we're talking about here."

"Everyone's not perfect like you, and I don't know how many times I've told you, a man is going to be a man, and that includes your man. Shit, these days a petty sexual indiscretion is nothing to march down to divorce court over. Whatever he can do, you can do."

"Petty?" Payton's response clarified why Sydney was reluctant to talk about this with her. She knew how Payton would react, but right now she'd had nowhere else to go. "Give me your damn laptop and let me show you petty."

"It's on the desk in my office. You go get the laptop and I'm going to go get me another sidecar and you a glass of wine. You need to relax," she mumbled as she retreated to the bar. She couldn't believe Sydney was this upset over Donathan's shenanigans. Frankly, she didn't know what reality her friend lived in. If she ever listened to her husband and those sexual exchanges on the radio, she would have seen this coming a mile away. Sydney needed to face the facts: Her man was fine, a local celebrity, and he didn't have to work too hard to attract the attention of women . . . and it was paying off for him.

Sydney returned with the laptop, typed in karma.com, and waited for the images to populate the screen. The guest intercom system, chimed. Payton yelled to her from the other room.

"Can you get that? Do you want red or white? How about a Hennessey bramble, like me?"

"I'll try a Hennessey bramble," she said, pressing the remote that was sitting on the table in front of her.

"Yes?"

"Ma'am, I have an Anthony Barnes down here, requesting entrance to your residence."

Sydney was silent, her anger fighting its way to the surface. What did Donathan hope to gain by sending Tony over to talk with her? She wasn't a child and refused to listen to another grown man plead Donathan's case, and as soon as he got up there she planned to tell him just that.

"Ma'am, is it okay to send the gentleman up?"

"That's fine."

Sydney placed the laptop on the table and went into the bathroom. She wanted this day to rewind, but she knew there was no such thing as a do-over. Her eyes were puffy, and the last thing she wanted was for Tony to report back to Donathan that she'd been crying. She gently splashed cold water onto her face repeatedly until it made her eyes sting. Through squinting eyes, she grabbed a paper towel and blotted her skin dry. Her reflection came into focus. No amount of cold water was going to fix her bloodshot eyes.

Payton sauntered out of the kitchen, two drinks in hand, and heard a light tapping at her front door. "Oh great," she practically shouted. Just what she needed—another uninvited visitor stopping by to put another wrinkle in her perfectly orgasmic plans. She hoped it was Donathan coming to collect his wife and leave her to her vices.

"I'm coming." She placed the drinks down on the table and headed for the front door. She opened the door, half-expecting Donathan, but saw a smiling Tony instead.

"You?" She turned on her heels and walked away from him.

He stepped inside, closed the door, and trapped her body between him and the foyer entrance wall; he kissed her neck and nibbled on her ear.

"Didn't you miss me?"

"Ooo," she cooed. "That shit feels good."

Sydney marched back into the room, ready to do battle, but was confused by the scene that was playing out in front of her. "What the fuck is going on here?" she screamed, startling both Payton and Tony, who stepped back like he had touched hot fire. "I can't believe this shit. My life is falling apart and I'm surrounded by cheaters and fucking liars!"

"Sydney, it's not what you think—"

"Oh, save that shit for somebody else, because that is the second time somebody has told me that bullshit tonight. What gets me is why this has to be a fucking secret. We're all adults and have been friends for almost twenty years. The fact that you didn't trust me enough to share what's going on with you and your life speaks volumes. Two people who are supposed to love me are keeping secrets . . . I am so fucking naïve," she said as she grabbed her purse and rushed past the twosome frozen in the entrance.

"I left the 'petty indiscretion' up on your laptop; please share it with Tony, but then again, who am I kidding, he probably already knew about that shit long before some photographer took those pictures," she said and slammed the door behind her.

Payton rushed over to the table and picked up her laptop. She shook her head and sighed heavily. She clicked the link and saw the pictures of Donathan and some woman, kissing at Mimosa. Tony scowled and then positioned the screen so he could get a better view.

"Why the hell is he in a lip lock with the fucking stalker?"

Chapter 27

With Tyrese's cell phone held tightly in her grasp, Joi tiptoed into the master bathroom and closed the door behind her. The family had been back from the camping trip at East Park Reservoir for less than twenty-four hours, and the humming of that damn phone had kept her awake for most of the night. After the incident at Eli's Mile High Club, Tyrese came home with the story that his truck had been vandalized and towed to the shop for repair. Joi went along with the lies, all the while planning her next move.

She locked the door, engaged the overhead fan, and typed in the password Tyrese had no idea she knew. The screen came to life, and she tapped on the message envelope to view his text messages.

There were ten from a woman named Debbie. The first texts were single sentences, things like, **Hey** and **Where are you?** but they escalated, each one seeming more desperate than the last. **You better not be trying to play me and Don't make me show up at your house because I do know where you live.** Joi's jaw tightened. The bitch had better think twice before rolling up to her front door. She wondered if Holsey had collected enough information on this tramp yet.

After seeing Holsey at Eli's, she'd felt confident that she was getting her money's worth, though with all her snooping she'd practically done the job for him. The only thing she hadn't known before today was the woman's name, and now she knew that, too. It had taken everything in her not to disclose to Tyrese that she knew about his little fling, but that information was her trump card. She just needed to get the physical proof from Holsey. Later today she'd call and make arrangements to meet with him.

Next, Joi pressed the voice-mail icon on the screen; it populated with a list of voice-mail messages waiting to be heard. She scrolled down as far as she could and saw every message was from the same number—Debbie's. She pressed Play and listened to the first message: "T, baby, where are you? I need you to—"

"Mommy, are you in there?" one of the twins asked, knocking on the door.

"Fuck," Joi mumbled under her breath. She ended the call and locked the screen.

"Mommmmmmmy," he called out again.

"Um, yes, baby. Mommy is in here having private time. I need you to be really quiet and not wake up Daddy. Go downstairs and Mommy will be right down to make you some red velvet pancakes."

"Yippee," she heard him squeal as he scurried away.

She sat there on the toilet seat for a moment and then, holding her breath, eased back into the master suite. She exhaled when she saw that Tyrese was still snoring, showing no sign of waking up anytime soon. She approached his nightstand and reconnected the phone to the charger. He stirred, and she hurried over to the window, and pretended to be adjusting the curtains to let in a bit of morning sunlight.

She stood there a moment and stared out the window, reflecting on the past week and how she had found the inner strength to keep her emotions in check. Camping had given her an opportunity to bond with her family, away from the outside world and its distractions. Her thoughts were interrupted by Tyrese, who pulled her into bed on top of him. When he kissed the side of her neck, she tensed.

"Morning, baby," he said, the extra bass still present in his voice. He slept in the raw and his morning wood was standing at attention.

"Why are you out of bed so early?" he asked, wrapping his arms around her waist and nuzzling his head against her curly mane. She put her game face on and turned to look at him.

"I was about to go downstairs to cook you some breakfast; then I thought we could hang out here in bed today and—"

He kissed her full on the lips. "Sweetheart, I can't do that today. You know it's my golf Saturday. I have to meet Donathan and Tony at eleven."

Joi stiffened. "We haven't even finished unpacking the truck. Can't you cancel today?" she whined like one of her four-year-olds. Her words were muffled in the crease of his neck.

He cupped her face with both hands and rested his forehead on hers. "Why don't you see if you can get your mother to keep the boys overnight, and when I get back from playing golf and running a few errands this afternoon, we can do whatever you like." He kissed her on the lips again and playfully slapped her on her ass. "Now go on and fix me something to eat."

Tyrese was a little perplexed as Joi scooted out of bed, grabbed her robe, and headed downstairs to the kitchen. Usually he had to work a little harder to settle her down, but she'd accepted his offer with little pushback. Maybe he was getting better at this. She'd barely left the room before he grabbed his phone off the nightstand and powered it on to listen to his voice mail. His body flushed as he listened to message after message from Debbie. He was tired of her little temper tantrums and he was going to put an end to this shit today. But it was the last message, the one from Curtis Holsey that really pissed him off. According to Curtis, Tyrese had until five o'clock today to take care of the arrangements they had discussed, and if Holsey didn't hear from him, he would assume it was okay to share the information he had gathered with Joi. Tyrese couldn't believe the frail motherfucker had the audacity to threaten him. And he planned to share with the little man just how much he hated threats when they met that afternoon.

★ ★ ★

When Joi got downstairs, she whipped up a batch of pancakes for the boys, and now they were happily seated at the table, enjoying their red pancakes. Next, she stirred the special batch for Tyrese. Lately, she'd learned to turn her emotions on and off like a faucet, pretending to be unaware of all the secrets and lies her husband was keeping from her, when the truth was, she couldn't think of anything else. She folded the pecan pieces into the batter just the way he liked them and waited for the griddle to reach the necessary temperature.

Once she poured four circles onto the flat surface, she opened the kitchen cabinet and reached for the small bottle of ipecac she had stashed at the very back. She took out a small spouted ramekin and filled it with warm maple syrup. She smiled as she mixed in three heaping tablespoons of the sugary medicine and placed the syrup on the serving tray. This would keep his wandering ass at home.

After the pancakes were ready, she carried the full tray upstairs, making sure not to spill the juice. She entered the room to an empty bed and a running shower.

"Ty, I thought I was bringing you breakfast in bed," she called out sweetly, feeling excited about her plan coming to fruition. After he got over the initial nausea, he would be fine and at home with her and the kids, where he belonged.

"Set the tray on the bed. I'll get it when I get out of the shower," he called out over the running water.

"But I cooked you red velvet pancakes with extra pecans, just the way you like them, and they're going to be cold," she said, balancing the tray on one arm, using the fork to stir the syrup inside the ramekin. "The least you could do is eat them, after I went to all the trouble—"

The shower turned off, and a few seconds later a wet Tyrese joined her in the bedroom with a white towel wrapped haphazardly around his waist. Joi smiled and held the tray. He kissed her, then sat down on the bed, and she placed the full tray on his lap.

He picked up the knife and fork and sliced the stack of pancakes into six pieces. He drowned the perfect triangles in the maple syrup and began eating.

"Umm," he said, taking another huge bite. "Baby, these are always so good. What do you put in these?"

"Nothing but love." She smiled. Joi watched him eat and realized she had plenty to think about before making any rash moves. She didn't know who he thought he was fooling. She could feel it in her gut that those errands he thought he was going to run today included Debbie—and that was something she had to put a stop to.

Tyrese ate his breakfast, dressed, and left the house in a hurry to make the standing tee time. He had hardly merged his SUV onto I-80 E when the sudden urge to vomit overcame him. He pulled over on the shoulder, opened the car door, and spilled his breakfast on the pavement. He retched continuously for almost ten minutes before the nausea subsided.

When he pulled into the parking lot of the Richmond Country Club, his heart was pounding fast, as if it wanted to jump out of his chest. Another wave of nausea hit him and he found himself standing next to his truck, dry heaving, which was where Donathan found him.

"Are you all right?"

"Man, I'm o—erup . . . erup."

Donathan stood helpless as he watched his friend retch. He looked at his watch. "I think we should cancel our game today." They stood there a while longer, and when Tyrese stood erect, his breathing hadn't slowed to normal. "I don't know what's wrong with me. I was fine when I left the house; then on my way here I had to pull over, and I've been upchucking ever since."

"Was it something you ate?"

"I had red velvet pancakes . . . nothing out of the ordinary. Maybe a bug I picked up on the camping trip." He wiped his mouth with the back of his hand. "Where's Tony?"

"His mother isn't doing well so he won't be joining us today."

Tyrese walked back to his truck, his heart palpitations echoing in his ears. He reached inside his car door, grabbed a package of wet wipes from the door pocket, and wiped his face and hands.

"C'mon, let's go inside and sit down for a minute. Maybe some club soda will settle your stomach."

Once inside, Tyrese excused himself to the men's room, returning some minutes later to the table overlooking the greens. His normally sparkling gray eyes were now a cold steel gray.

"Are you feeling any better?" Donathan asked.

"Still a little nauseated," he said, pulling out his chair and taking a seat. "Man, I just don't understand it. I felt perfectly fine when I left the house and then all of a sudden I felt like my insides were clawing their way out."

"Well, whatever you've got I don't need." Donathan chuckled and scooted his chair a little farther from the table. "What's on your agenda for the rest of the day?"

"Man, you won't believe this shit. The other night I was at Eli's Mile High Club on MLK with the temp. I was approached by a private investigator who'd been hired by Joi to confirm her suspicions that I was cheating on her. He offered to destroy his photo evidence if I gave him twenty-five hundred dollars."

"So what did you do?"

"I haven't done anything yet. He left me a message this morning threatening to tell Joi if I didn't pay him by five o'clock today. And that's not the worst of it."

"Go on."

"That broad Debbie has turned into my worst nightmare. The girl is calling me night and day, asking for money—she wants twelve hundred dollars to buy a purse, and frankly, I'm tired of her shit, too. After our meeting, I agreed to meet her outside of work and I was going to give her the money if that was going to keep her ass quiet. But when we got back to my truck, all my tires had been slashed. Fucking ghetto-ass neighborhood. I had to call Triple A. They towed my shit to Firestone in Richmond and dropped me off at home. That broad has left me twenty-two messages in the past twenty-four hours, and in the last one she threatened to come to my house if I didn't call her back."

"Man, I told you to be careful. Once they start showing up at your house, it's only a matter of time before your wife finds out."

Tyrese looked at Donathan, really looked at him, then said, "You sound like a man speaking from experience."

"Yes, actually, I am. Sydney left me last night."

"You got to be fucking kidding me. What happened?"

"A few weeks back I met this red-boned chick here at the bar. We hooked up later that night at Maxwell's, and to make a long story short, she slipped me some roofies or something and did God knows what to me, took pictures, showed up at my office, and at my house. I can't even shit right now without this woman knowing about it. The bitch is stalking me."

"Drugged you? Showed up at your house?"

"And that's not the half of it. She's had run-ins with my neighbors. Compared to Austyn, Debbie sounds like a walk in the park. Austyn didn't threaten; she just showed up and left me with the mess to deal with after she was gone." He glanced around, as if expecting her to walk in at any moment.

"So why did Sydney leave you?"

"See, that's the thing: I've been racking my brain, trying to outsmart this chick, and she seems to be one step ahead of me. I met her at Mimosa's the other night, hoping I could learn more about her so I could figure out why she's fixated on me. But instead of walking away with solid information, I ended up as the lead on karma.com, in a serious lip lock with the woman. Sydney saw it, and let's just say she's not a happy camper."

"Look at you, man; you don't look like you're losing any sleep. I mean, your wife has left you and you've got a psycho bitch puppeteering your life, but you look as fresh as a cucumber. What gives?"

"Actually, it's better for me that Sydney is gone. Let her cool off at Payton's for a few days and I can concentrate on finding Austyn and getting to the bottom of everything."

"See, this is why I'm going to pay Debbie a visit today. Something has to be done about these women. They overstep their bounds and need to be put in check."

"What about the private investigator?"

"Man, I want to whoop his old shriveled-up ass, but I can't deal with him on that level right now. The best thing for me to do is to pay that motherfucker and walk away."

Donathan nodded. "Sometimes it's best to cut bait, especially if that means your wife won't have to find out about your indiscretions."

"Exactly, which is why I'm about to get on up the road and take care of my two little problems. Then I'm back to the house to settle my wife down," he said in a serious tone. "The last thing I need is for her to go rogue."

Chapter 28

After slamming the door at Payton's condo the night before, Sydney had made her way to the Waterfront Hotel. She'd tossed and turned for most of the night, confused about how she should handle her situation with Donathan. She gazed out her hotel window, ruminating on the state of her life; from where she stood, things were pretty messed up.

Earlier, she'd put on her running shoes and run until she couldn't run anymore. But the confusion taking up space in her head ran right alongside her like a running partner, yammering to her with every footfall that struck the pavement.

A light tap at her door startled her. When she looked through the small peephole, she almost passed out. Miles was the last person she expected to see. She had spoken with him briefly last night, after she left Payton's. He had wanted to meet her, but she'd assured him she was okay and planned to check into the Waterfront.

"What are you doing here?" she questioned, her body blocking the opening in the door.

"I was in the neighborhood and thought I'd check on you. I thought maybe I could take you out to grab a bite to eat or maybe just talk," he said, his voice trailing off. She looked down at her sports attire and brushed her hand across her hair, still damp with perspiration from her run.

"Did you think about calling first?" she said, perplexed by his presence.

"I did that all morning and I didn't get an answer or return call, so here I am."

Then she remembered that she had not taken anyone's calls. She wished she could just turn it off, but being just a phone call away was one of the burdens of being a doctor.

There was an awkward silence as they stared at one another. Sydney wanted to be left alone with her thoughts.

"I'm not taking no for an answer," he said, shifting his weight. "If you don't want to talk, that's fine with me, but you do have to eat."

She stepped to the side and allowed him entry into her space.

"Wait here and I'll go get cleaned up."

As she showered, her body felt heavy with despair. She scrutinized the situation in her head, again trying to apply her logic, searching for any reason that would justify Donathan's behavior. But she kept arriving at the same conclusion: Her husband was a fucking cheater and he had humiliated her. It was one thing for a woman to find out about her husband's infidelities when no one knew except her, her husband, and the other woman. In those cases, most women made dumb decisions and went back to their men. But when your shit was plastered on the internet for all to see, your actions and reactions would be scrutinized in the public arena. This added a different layer. She wasn't the "good wife" and didn't feel obligated to stand by her man like he was the second coming. The pictures were worth a thousand words, and Sydney knew this was probably just the tip of the iceberg.

After putting on a simple chic sundress, Sydney wandered back into the sitting area, where Miles was in a cheerful mood. She gave him an appraising glance. He had on freshly starched jeans, hard-sole loafers, and a striped light blue and white button-down that gently grabbed his well-defined biceps.

"Are you ready to go?"

Sydney nodded her head.

"You like seafood, don't you?"

"Of course." She grabbed her tote from the table.

"Good. I made us a reservation at a restaurant in Half Moon Bay."

They walked down the three flights of stairs past the entrance to Miss Pearl's Jam House and exited through the automatic doors. As they approached the valet station, Sydney fumbled through her tote and glanced at her cell phone again. She frowned and placed it back into her purse.

Miles asked, "Have you two talked about it?"

His jet-black Viper was parked in the paved turnabout. The valet opened the passenger door for Sydney and then the driver's side door for Miles. Once inside the confines of the car, she replied, "Briefly."

"Do you want to talk about it?"

Sydney shifted in her seat. Talking about Donathan was the last thing she wanted to do. She turned away. Before she'd taken her shower, she'd checked her cell phone for messages. There were none from Donathan. The fact that she'd been gone overnight and he hadn't bothered to call or come looking for her only confirmed that her decision to leave had been the right one.

"You know what, why don't we make Donathan off limits this afternoon?" Miles said, as if he'd read her mind. "I'm sure we can find something else to talk about."

They drove down Highway 1 along the Pacific Ocean's edge. The view was breathtaking; exactly what Sydney needed to help to clear her head. After an hour or so they ended up at Sam's Chowder House, where they enjoyed the New England–style clambake filled with Maine lobster, mussels, corn on the cob, red potatoes, and sausage. Unfortunately, Sydney washed it down with a lot of wine. After their meal they sat by the firepots, enjoying the view, but when they left Half Moon Bay, Sydney was drunk.

An hour and a half later, when they pulled back into the Waterfront Hotel, Sydney was still buzzed. She hated the fact that she'd had too much to drink. Miles ushered her through a side door and this time they took the elevator to the third floor. In the midst of going through her purse in search of the room's key card, Sydney dropped the bag and spilled the contents on the floor. "Uh-oh." Sydney giggled.

"Let's get you inside." Miles helped her to the couch, then returned to the hallway to retrieve her things.

Sydney's head was spinning. Donathan had always teased her about her low tolerance for alcohol, calling her a cheap date. Normally she could drink two full glasses of Chardonnay and be fine, but she'd known she was way past her limit when she'd downed that fourth glass. But she had wanted to forget the past forty-eight hours. She wanted to erase them by drinking until she couldn't remember.

Miles returned. He helped her into the adjoining bedroom, placed her on the king-size bed, and covered her with a lightweight blanket. She closed her eyes as her dulled senses took over. All she could see was her husband kissing that woman, and that made her want to cry. He'd promised before God and her daddy to love and be faithful to her.

"I'm thirsty. Can I have some more wine?"

"Oh, I think you've had enough wine for today. How about some water?"

Miles returned to the front room to make sure the lock on the door was secured and to get Sydney a bottle of water. When he reentered the bedroom, she was sprawled across the bed and had managed to twist herself in her dress, which looked very uncomfortable. She was fast asleep.

She stirred briefly as Miles worked to remove her dress, which was tangled under her arms. He waited for her breathing to resume a measured cadence before easing her dress down past her petite hips and bare legs. He felt like a voyeur, staring at her half-naked body, her breasts rising and falling in a slow, easy rhythm. She had on the prettiest underwear that contrasted nicely against her smooth brown skin. The bra was a coral mesh with a contrasting animal print trim that matched her panty. Sydney moaned softly when he eased her between the sheets.

"Miles."

"Yes, Sydney?"

"I'm sorry . . . please don't leave me."

He paused before he removed his shoes and eased into the bed beside her. Pressing his chest to her back, he rested his arm across her waist and pulled her closer.

"I'm sorry, too, sweetheart," he whispered. "I'm right here."

Chapter 29

When Payton arrived at Picán, a well-dressed gentleman opened the door and smiled as she swept through the restaurant entrance.

Along with two women, David Bryant was sitting at the bar doing what he did best—flirting. But as far as Payton was concerned, why not make use of any connections he could muster? David wasn't just another handsome face. He owned multiple car dealerships, but he also had charisma, charm, and, most importantly, the swagger of a man who had deep pockets.

They were seated at a window table for two in the Bourbon Room, near the back of the restaurant. As usual, Payton made sure she was seated facing the front door, with an unobstructed view of everyone who entered and exited, which was something she did whenever she was out in public with a married man. That way, if any significant others showed up, she'd see them coming without being ambushed. The burlap sheers covering the floor-to-ceiling windows and the minimal recessed lighting gave Picán a warm and cozy feel.

David snapped his fingers for the waiter, who was dressed all in black except for a chocolate apron cinched at his waist. "Would you like a drink?" he asked.

Payton sat up straighter and pondered the question for a second. She found herself overwhelmed with a rush of bad memories from the incident with Sydney and her bout with those Hennessey sidecars last night. They'd left her with a lingering headache for most of the morning, so her plan for tonight was to drink light. She'd left multiple messages for Sydney last night and today and still hadn't heard from her. She didn't understand what the big deal was. So what if she was fucking Tony? She was a grown-ass woman who could fuck whomever she pleased and wasn't obligated to share that information with anyone.

Once Sydney had left, Tony had kissed her ass and of course he'd explained why he hadn't returned her calls in four days. Something about a broken phone and his mother being moved to hospice, but life was too short to wait around for grown-ass men. After she thought about it, she concluded it really didn't matter why Tony hadn't returned her calls. The fact of the matter was, he hadn't. And she wasn't about to wait around and get caught up for any man.

"A glass of Riesling," she said finally, feeling David's eyes on her.

"What's the matter? Afraid I'll take advantage of you if you get something a little stronger?" David said, narrowing his gaze.

"I don't need alcohol to let you take advantage of me."

"Touché," he said and chuckled.

The easy sound soothed Payton's ears, and a few minutes later the waiter returned with her Riesling and a small plate with four pieces of corn bread and some honey-whipped butter. Payton ordered a Southern Caesar with shrimp and grits and David ordered the Berkshire pork chops.

After the server left, David reached across the table and took her free hand in his. "You know you're like a drug; you can't get a brotha hooked and then make him go cold turkey."

Payton smiled, toying with David's assessment. No one had ever called her a drug, but when it came to sex, she knew she had skills... the kind that could become very habit-forming. She'd had a few friends with benefits in her past who couldn't seem to let go, but David wasn't one of them. He intrigued her. She'd met him at a charity function a few years before and they'd been friends ever since.

"So here we are," he said, bringing her hand to his mouth. He kissed it slowly, wiggling his tongue between her fingers. "Especially after you left me high and dry last night."

Payton smiled again but still wasn't ready to show any of the excitement she felt. She took a sip of the pale liquid.

He released her hand, leaned back in his chair, and slowly stroked his goatee. "What color panty do you have on?"

"Well, if you play your cards right, maybe I'll let you take a peek."

He smeared a piece of the corn bread and fed it to Payton, who let the tips of his fingers linger in her mouth. Her eyes were glued to his as she watched him take his fingers back to his own lips and seductively lick each one.

Payton was so busy enjoying the show, she was unaware of a stilled silhouette that peered at her from outside the window. A few seconds passed before she finally glanced his way. She looked once, twice, three times, and as he raised his retro Ray-Bans, it struck her. His bloodshot eyes pierced a hole through her and she sucked in air as a guilty expression washed over her face. She forgot to breathe. Tony lowered the glasses and retraced his steps as he walked away.

David looked on, taking notice of her agitation. She downed the rest of her wine and immediately motioned to the waiter for a second glass.

"Is that somebody important to you?" David asked with sincere concern.

"He used to be, but not anymore."

Chapter 30

Staring at herself in the mirror, Payton was conflicted. She would have preferred another color, but she dressed down, all in black, out of respect for a woman she'd never had the opportunity to meet.

Half of her wanted to hide in her condo and not give a damn about Tony and what he was going through. The other half wanted to face the world and say *fuck 'em all*, as she was so prone to do.

But could she maintain her façade when she saw him? She hadn't spoken to Tony since the incident at Picán last Saturday night, and her stomach was doing flipflops.

A few nights after he'd walked away from the window at Picán she'd called him. His voice mail was full, and before she lost her nerve, she'd called his home. Najee, his sister, had answered, shared with Payton that their mother had passed, and provided her with the funeral service information. Payton wrestled back and forth with herself as to why she should attend the service and finally settled on the fact that if nothing else, she considered Tony her friend. Even though the look on his face after he saw her with David said otherwise, she knew this was the right thing to do.

Once inside the sanctuary, Payton deliberately took a seat in the back pew. She wished Sydney were there with her to bolster her confidence. The bevy of brown UPS uniforms in every size, shape, and color were everywhere. She felt like she was at an all-you-can-eat smorgasbord.

A light tap on her shoulder startled her. She looked up into the face of Sydney and Donathan's nosy-ass neighbor, Mrs. Brown. She gave the older lady a once-over, taking in her sequined black ballet slippers and a ruffled black dress that made her look twice her size. She looked a hot mess.

"Baby, why are you sitting back here all by yourself? There's plenty of room up there," she said, pointing toward some empty seats at the front of the church.

"How did you know Sister Shirley? She was such a lovely woman. I'm so sad to see her life cut short, but glory be to God because he knows best."

Donathan walked through the sanctuary and nearly bumped into his neighbor, Barbara Brown. She reached out and grabbed him by the arm before he could pass her by.

"Donathan James, is that you?"

He removed his sunglasses. "Mrs. Brown, what are you doing here?"

"Chile, I'm here to pay my respects to Sister Shirley."

"That's right; you and Mama Barnes were on several church auxiliaries together," he replied, finally noticing and nodding at Payton. "Mama Barnes mentioned to me that she knew one of my neighbors, but I hadn't put two and two together."

"Where's Sydney? Y'know I haven't seen her since she stormed out of the house about a week ago. Is she out of town on business again?"

Donathan's eyes darted left, then right, as he tried to think of something to say to appease her.

"I've been meaning to come over and talk to both of you. I think I saw that crazy gal parked in front of your house again on Sunday evening. I heard someone laughing like a hyena and peeped outside the front window. I went to fetch my glasses, but when I returned, she was gone. I know it was her, and you better be careful, because something's just not right about that chile. I told Herbert the next time I see her ova there I would call the police."

"Mrs. Brown, you didn't happen to get the license plate number on her car, did you?"

"I sure did," she said, nodding her head like he should have known better than to ask her that question. "As the head of our neighborhood watch committee, I write down any suspicious activity I see in the neighborhood. I've had the license plate number to the car since that gal came over the second time. I was going to give it to you, but when she said she was a friend of yours, I didn't think you needed it. I wrote it down just in case."

"Have you told Sydney any of this?" he said, pretending to be confused. He'd been trying to make amends with his wife without much success. He was well aware how furious she was when she'd left and had been apprehensive about facing her because he still didn't have any answers, but Mrs. Brown was about to change that for him. He didn't know why he hadn't thought about this sooner. For once, this meddling woman was the answer to his prayers.

"No, I haven't. Herbert told me to stay out of folks' business. Y'know, Donathan, we women can sense when things just ain't right, and that crazy gal has got *wrong* stamped across her forehead. I told Herbert if she was your friend, why did she need to be so sneaky, hand-delivering packages and leaving them inside the gate?"

"Mrs. Brown, how can I get the license plate number from you?"

"I have it at home on my watch log. I won't be home until later this evening because I'll be serving food at the repast. But as soon as I get home, I can bring it over to you."

"Why don't you just call me when you get in and I'll come over to get it? But in the meantime, when you see Sydney today, can you share the information about the woman with her?" he said, trying not to get ahead of himself. A full license-plate number was the jackpot.

Mrs. Brown paused for a moment, looking confused. "Is everything okay, baby?"

"Everything is fine."

"Well, most of the time folks don't want me to discuss what I see."

"Everything is fine, but it would really help me a lot if you shared the information with Sydney when you see her today." The more he thought about it, the more he thought having Mrs. Brown tell Sydney about Austyn was the smart thing to do. He could play dumb, and when Mrs. Brown did what she did best, he would come out smelling like a rose.

"All right, baby, I can do that for you," she said before she walked away.

Payton couldn't believe what she'd overheard. She needed to talk to Sydney. In Payton's opinion, Sydney was taking this too far. Because she hadn't returned any of Payton's calls since she'd stormed out of her condo on Friday, Payton had assumed Sydney had gone home, but from the sound of things, home wasn't where she'd been laying her head. That was almost a week ago. After the services were over, she planned to hunt her down and have a serious face-to-face talk with her.

"Will everyone please take your seats so the family can be seated?" a tall, slender man wearing a dark suit, a crisp white shirt, and a black tie announced.

Within seconds, Payton's problem was solved when Sydney entered the sanctuary. She, too, was dressed in black, with her favorite teardrop diamond necklace nestled at her neck. She made brief eye contact with Payton and then continued a few rows up, taking a seat in the opposite pew.

"Hello to you, too," Payton mumbled sarcastically.

Everyone took their seats and six pallbearers, including Donathan and Tyrese, walked down the aisle in a nestled group. Once they were seated in the row directly behind the row reserved for family, Tony, along with a young teenage girl Payton presumed to be Najee and an older woman clinging to his arm were escorted down the center aisle.

The funeral service was short and dignified. Shirley Barnes didn't have a lot of immediate family and the majority of people in attendance were Tony's friends. Several church members gave eulogies and Tony finally made his way to the podium. All eyes were on him, including Payton's.

He spoke about his mother with great admiration, his words kind and gentle. She wasn't sure if he'd noticed her when he was escorted into the church; he hadn't acknowledged her. But all she wanted to do today was show some respect for his mother, and whether he spoke to her or not, she'd done what she'd been there to do.

CHAPTER 31

Joi almost tripped, the heel of her shoe stuck under a piece of linoleum. She scowled at the muted, brown-paneled waiting area of Holsey Investigations, riddled with scarred, mismatched chairs, dilapidated flooring, and three brown picture frames mounted on the one sand-colored wall that displayed the words *Reliable, Trustworthy,* and *Confidential* written in gold.

She took a seat in one of the mismatched chairs, in turmoil. When she'd initially started this expedition, she'd thought she knew exactly what she would do if she found out Tyrese was cheating on her. Now she wasn't so sure about her impending decision. This meeting with Holsey was just a formality because she'd confirmed her suspicions already, but now everything wasn't so cut and dried. The attorney had said she needed proof if she wanted a divorce; now she wasn't sure.

"Mrs. White, Mr. Holsey will be right with you. He's running a little behind schedule this afternoon."

Joi looked at her watch. There was no preschool today; she'd gotten one of the playgroup moms to keep an eye on the boys for a few hours during her annual gynecology appointment and now they were with her mother. She needed to get back home soon.

"Um, how much longer do you think he'll be?" she questioned the matronly receptionist.

"Not long, Mrs. White. I'm sure he'll be done soon."

Joi picked up an outdated copy of *People* magazine and nervously thumbed through the pages, attempting to read an article on infidelity as she waited, but she was anxious and distracted. What was she going to do if the PI had gathered more incriminating evidence on her husband? She loved him so much; she always had.

She'd given Tyrese the ipecac twice, like she'd read about on the internet, but it hadn't had any effect on him. It was supposed to make him feel nauseous, and she'd hoped he would opt to stay home instead of running the streets. But he never showed any signs of sickness. Maybe she hadn't used enough. If it wasn't for that bitch Debbie, who was waiting in the wings to fuck his brains out at every opportunity, he would be home. Her thoughts grew increasingly paranoid as she returned the magazine to the circular table and picked up another outdated copy.

She heard a door open and noticed a young woman who looked a lot like her walk past. The woman's huge diamond ring sparkled, but what caught Joi's attention was the manila envelope tucked underneath her arm. The receptionist interrupted her thoughts.

"Mrs. White, Mr. Holsey will see you now."

Joi watched until the previous client was out the front door before she stood and moved toward the inner office. She stepped through the doorway and started toward a putty colored metal chair.

"Sorry to keep you waiting," Holsey croaked, and motioned for her to close the office door behind her. He sat behind a metal desk littered with mounds of file folders and paper. Before Joi took a seat, she tried to make eye contact to search for a clue to the outcome of this meeting, but she couldn't get a read on the man. His eyes shifted back and forth as he puffed on a cigarette and stared down at the stack of papers. Joi coughed and fanned the air in front of her. If he had something to give her, she wanted to make it quick; the last thing she needed was to let the smoke permeate her clothes. She didn't want to return home smelling like an ashtray. She shifted in her seat and coughed again. Holsey extinguished his cigarette and opened one of the green files.

"Mrs. White, I've run several surveillance operations on your husband since you hired me and I'm happy to report that I didn't find an ounce of evidence to support your suspicions. Now, unfortunately, in my line of work, I don't get to say this to all my clients, but if I were you, I'd end my snooping and be happy you have a good man."

Joi stared at Holsey, not believing what she'd just heard. Did he just say he didn't find an ounce of evidence? He had to be mistaken. She'd seen him and Tyrese with her own eyes at Eli's.

"Now, I do have a few additional expenses and I hope we can clear them up immediately," Holsey said. He closed the first file and opened another one.

Was he asking for more money? This had to be a joke. Her eyes narrowed as Holsey put on a pair of reading glasses and ran his arthritic index finger across the coffee-stained page in front of him.

"Looks like about five hundred dollars will make us even," he said, a smile playing at the corners of his lips for the first time.

This wasn't turning out like she'd planned. When she'd hired him, of course, she wanted him to say he found nothing and her husband was a good man, but that was her dream, before she'd seen the truth with her own eyes.

Joi jumped from her seat. "You lying son of a bitch."

Holsey cleared his throat, a strange look in his eyes. "Excuse me?" His tone was icy.

Joi leaned across the desk, within inches of his face. "I saw you. I can't believe you're lying to my face. I saw you and my no-good-ass husband, Tyrese White, with that bitch. And now you're telling me there was no evidence. Look here, Mr. Holsey, I don't know what kind of game you're running, but you won't be running it on me. If you know what's good for you, you'd better get out your checkbook, or better yet one of those envelopes you keep in your glove box, and give me my goddamn money back or else," she said, standing erect and folding her arms across her body.

Holsey stood, his smile and confidence wavering. "I'm not sure what you think you saw, but—"

"Mr. Holsey, is everything all right in there? You don't need me to call the police, do you?" the matronly receptionist called out, her voice muffled by the closed door.

There was a stare down and a long silence. "The police won't be necessary, Wilma," he said, never taking his eyes off Joi. He retrieved an envelope from the top right desk drawer.

Joi chewed on her bottom lip as he counted out fifty crisp one-hundred-dollar bills and thrust them in her direction. "You take this money and get the hell out of my office," he said, a sharp edge to his raspy voice.

"You can't possibly be serious." Joi yanked the money from his grasp. She folded it in half and tucked it into the side pocket of her purse. "I should report you to the police and anyone else who will listen." Turning on her heel, she opened the door on the stunned receptionist, who was standing there with her ear glued to the door.

With her thoughts racing in a hundred different directions, none of them good, Joi brushed past her and stormed out to her car. Getting the five thousand dollars back was something she hadn't expected, but right now the money was the least of her worries. Her dilemma was what she was going to do about her cheating husband.

Donathan was standing outside Holsey's office building, talking to Tyrese on his phone when he noticed Joi hurrying toward her SUV. She looked upset and zoned out of her surroundings as she slid into the driver's seat.

"Your wife is leaving his office right now," Donathan whispered into the phone.

"I know. That bastard told me he was meeting with her today, after I gave him my twenty-five hundred dollars. And he had the nerve to want cash," Tyrese grumbled.

"When you told me you were being shaken down by a private detective, I didn't know it was the one I'd hired. Man, he'd better not even think about taking me for money."

"He better have kept his word because I want to kick his ass so bad right now I barely need a reason. I just want this shit to be over."

"Well, Joi looked pissed, so I bet their exchange was heated. I couldn't hear what she was saying, but I could hear voices in the reception area and they didn't sound nice. Did you get the situation with Debbie straightened out?"

"Threw some money at that problem on Saturday. It's all good."

Donathan shook his head. The worst thing Tyrese could have done was start giving that chick money. Now she was going to treat him like a twenty-four-hour ATM machine.

"I hate to burst your bubble, but I wouldn't count on it," Donathan said, moving toward the waving receptionist. He stepped into the building. "Got a strong hunch you haven't seen the last of her."

"What do you mean?" Tyrese responded.

Donathan couldn't believe his friend was this clueless. "Look, I gotta run, but you're a smart man. Figure it out."

Chapter 32

For the first time since Payton could remember, the house on 12th Street was devoid of any activity. She'd arrived a half hour early to take her final walk-through before the real estate investors got there. The smell of the newly varnished hardwood floors stirred up childhood memories that made her smile, but thoughts of her mother lingered on the fringe of her mind and had plagued her since her uncle had mentioned she'd been back around. But Payton knew as well as anyone that when a drug-addicted family member reappeared after a long absence, it could only mean one thing: her mother wanted something.

Payton paused on the stairs and admired the bright white crown molding between the white ceiling and taupe walls, an accent Tony had suggested. This simple architectural touch nestled around the ceiling, giving the room an elegant and regal feel. When she reached the last step, leading from the upstairs bedrooms, a kernel of an idea came to her. Yesterday Sydney had tried to avoid her like the plague. After the viewing procession, instead of being ushered back to her seat for the remainder of the funeral service, she'd slipped out the side door, but Payton had anticipated her move and cornered her outside the church. Sydney rushed past her, claiming she had to get back to the hospital, but they'd been friends for a long time and Payton could feel in her gut that she was lying. She imagined her and Tony being friends again. She missed their easy conversation, and if she was honest with herself, the thought of not having sex with him again would be a huge disappointment. He hadn't even tried to contact her since the incident at Picán. He must still be upset about that.

Payton removed her phone from her purse and with a few upward swipes located Tony's number, then pressed Enter.

"Hello?"

She eased down on the stairs, her voice caught in her throat. She'd hoped he would answer the phone, but she was caught off guard just the same.

"Hello?" he repeated, his tone ice-cold. "Who is this?" he barked before she finally found her voice.

"What'd you do, erase my number from your contacts?" she asked, chuckling nervously. There was a long silence. "Is this a bad time?"

"No. What's up?"

"I . . . I didn't get the chance to offer you my condolences yesterday."

"Thanks," he said, less than enthusiastic.

"Have you spoken with Donathan?" Payton asked, thinking she needed to speed the conversation along.

"What kind of question is that? Of course I spoke to him."

"Did he say anything about Sydney?"

"What about Sydney?"

"Did you mention to him what happened the other night?" Payton inquired, growing tired of his pissy attitude. "I just thought you might want to help your friend."

"Payton, in case you haven't noticed, my friend is a grown-ass man. If he needed my help, he would ask. If I were you, I'd just stay out of it."

"What do you mean, stay out of it?"

"Donathan and Sydney are perfectly capable of figuring this

out by themselves. Look, Payton, I gotta go. I'm running late for an appointment."

"Wait a minute. We owe it to Sydney to make sure she knows the truth."

"She's your friend; why don't you handle that?"

"I thought it would be better coming from a man," Payton snapped back, knowing he was right.

"Me? Oh, now I see what's going on. She must not be taking your calls."

"No, she's not. She hasn't been home since we saw her last."

"Like I told you, they need to work their situation out on their own."

"Well, what about our situation?" Payton asked, wanting to kick herself once the words left her lips. Tony didn't answer immediately; instead, he let her question hang in the air. Why the hell had she asked that question? She wanted to kick herself.

"Can you come by my place later so we can talk?" she said, sounding uncomfortable. "There's something I should explain to you about the other night."

"You don't have to explain anything to me. Why don't you call the dude who was sucking your fingers and probably fucking you the other night?"

"Excuse me, what did you just say? You have a lot of damn nerve talking to me like that. You and I have never agreed to be anything more than being friends, and now you want to show your ass because you saw me with a friend. Ain't that about a bitch? And for the record, you are absolutely right. The dude I was with the other night won't have a problem feeding or fucking me." She ended the call.

"Fuck him!" she yelled out loud.

An hour later Payton stood on the front lawn, watching the retreating backs of the investors as they sank into the plush leather seats of their waiting car. Engrossed in her thoughts, she didn't notice the woman walking up behind her.

"Excuse me," the woman said, stopping within inches of Payton, who turned around and took her inventory. The woman was wearing jeans, high-heeled boots, and a short, stylish fox-fur vest, all simple and understated but collectively put at least one comma on a sales receipt. Her hair was an arresting red and she wore a pair of oversize sunglasses that obscured her striking beauty. But she looked familiar to Payton, nonetheless.

"I'm looking for Lois Greene."

Payton was overcome with feelings of deep apprehension. She hadn't heard anyone say that name out loud in years, and the mere mention of it sent her heart into overdrive. "Did you say Lois Greene?"

"Yes. This is the last address I was given for her."

"Well, there's nobody here by that name. Did Lois win the lottery or something?"

"Or something," the woman said, her face darkening with annoyance.

"Well, if I do see Ms. Greene around these parts, who shall I say stopped by?"

"You say Ms. Greene doesn't live here, so I don't think you'll need to tell her anything."

"Do I know you?" Payton interrupted, eyeing the woman suspiciously. "Who'd you say you were again?" she asked, knowing the woman hadn't given her a name.

There was a brief silence.

"I didn't say, and no, I'm afraid we've never met." She turned on her heel and never looked back as she retraced her steps to the edge of the lawn. Payton followed, perplexed because she knew she'd seen this woman before but couldn't place her. Recognition was standing between them like an elephant in the room. Except they weren't in a room and the woman was retreating briskly to a light blue Saturn parked a few doors down.

The woman eased behind the wheel of her car and glanced in Payton's direction one last time before driving away.

"Oh my God!" Payton roared as recognition set in. It was the woman from the karma.com pictures with Donathan. What the hell was she doing in Pittsburg? And what the hell did she want with Lois Greene?

Chapter 33

By the time Joi made it inside Starbucks, the rain had soaked her from head to toe. She took a seat at a small bistro table and took deep, cleansing breaths in an attempt to calm down and think rationally. John Coltrane's saxophone was blaring "In a Sentimental Mood" through the sound system, but despite the music, all she could hear was a loop of Dr. Hardy's voice saying, "You have chlamydia." She'd gone in for a routine exam and came out with a fucking sexually transmitted disease. How in the hell does a married woman in a monogamous relationship end up with a goddamn sexually transmitted disease?

She could feel the blood rushing to her face as her eyes filled with tears and began sliding down her cheeks. She shifted from the hip where she'd been given a penicillin injection and dialed Tyrese's office number again.

"Connie, is my husband available?" she asked, growing increasingly agitated.

"No, ma'am, he's *still* in that meeting with the general manager, but as soon as he gets back to his office, I *promise* to tell him to phone you."

Joi could tell by the way Connie emphasized the words *still* and *promise* that she'd grown tired of Joi's barrage of phone calls. But she didn't give a damn. She felt like driving to his office in East

Oakland and personally disturbing the meeting herself. If there even was a meeting.

"You make sure you do that," Joi hissed before she pressed the red button, sending the call into cell-phone oblivion. When she glanced up, several patrons were staring at her. With her lips twisted in an angry knot, she slammed her phone on the table and stared back.

"Are you okay?" asked an elderly woman who was dressed all in black, except for the hand-knitted raspberry beret tilted on her head.

"Mind your own damn business," Joi muttered as she massaged her now-pounding temples. *Please, God, help me,* she chanted in her head as a comforting mantra. She'd heard horror stories of infidelity from a few moms from the boys' playgroup, like the husband who'd arrived at the Oakland International Airport with his mistress only to find his wife waiting, and the husband who'd been caught in his master bedroom with another woman. She could even recall a few more, but she'd never heard of anyone catching an STD before. She was so confused and didn't know what to do.

Marrying Tyrese had afforded her a very comfortable lifestyle, one she had no intention of giving up. Apart from that, she had her children to consider—the victims in this complicated situation. Well, complicated only because her fucking husband couldn't keep his dick in his pants. From what Dr. Hardy had said, chlamydia was known as a silent disease because it wasn't uncommon for women to go around without symptoms, and in some instances men didn't have symptoms either. Joi couldn't believe he'd been treated for something that serious and hadn't told her. So, he had to be infected right now. He had to be confronted with the information she had.

She sighed heavily, feeling desperate because she really didn't have any concrete evidence of Tyrese's infidelity. And just like that, another thought occurred to her: Why was she sitting here acting like a victim? For once in her life she held all the cards, with her ace of spades being the chlamydia. She knew the chick he was fucking and where she lived. Feeling a rush of courage, she hesitated only briefly before she typed the words *moving company* into her iPhone. Once the screen filled up, she scrolled down the listing and picked one: Allied Movers.

Ten minutes later, clutching her raincoat around her, Joi hurried out of Starbucks. "Fucking bastard," she spat as she got into her SUV and headed home. She felt dirty and humiliated. What Tyrese had done sickened her—fooling around with some dirty whore—but she'd finally conjured up the nerve to do what she needed to do. She was leaving his ass.

By the time Joi made it home she was feeling pretty damned pleased with herself. The feeling lasted until she entered the home office; then all at once it seemed like the room was closing in on her, even more so with the picture of Tyrese and the boys staring back at her. With shaking hands, she opened the desk drawer, retrieved the credit card they used only to pay household bills, and dialed the movers she'd contacted before she'd left Starbucks.

"Now, are you sure you can finish this job by five o'clock today?" she asked after completing the credit card transaction. It was ten a.m. and she believed in the less-is-more philosophy when it came to furnishings. She didn't know where she would eventually land just yet, but she would place the furniture in storage and she and the boys would stay with her mom until she worked out a plan.

"Absolutely, ma'am," the guy on the phone responded. "The truck and the men are on their way."

"Good. Because I want them to pack up everything."

Tyrese exited the executive wing, stunned by the events that had transpired. Effective immediately, he'd been placed on administrative leave due to a sexual harassment complaint. Debbie had called him last night, asking for more money. She had threatened that he'd be sorry if he continued to ignore her, but he hadn't taken her seriously. Obviously a huge mistake. He stopped walking and stared at Debbie. She sported a new blond-colored weave; his gray eyes flashed danger. She'd cost him enough. Four punctured tires and twelve hundred dollars were plenty for that world-class blow job. She'd willingly sucked him dry, but now her ghetto ass was determined to screw everything up.

He spun on his soles and took long, deliberate strides toward his office. Before he reached his door his secretary called out to him.

"Excuse me, Mr. White, your wife called multiple times and—"

"Not now, Connie," he snapped, moving past her and slamming his office door behind him. His job would be in limbo for the next seven days while they investigated her claim.

"Fucking devious bitch," he muttered, pulling back the leather chair behind his desk and sitting down. When he picked up his cell phone he experienced a twinge of guilt as he noted the numerous missed calls from Joi. How would he explain his involuntary leave to her? He could continue to get up every morning and leave the house like he was going to work, but as much as Joi called him every day, that didn't seem like a good idea. He tossed around a few different scenarios before settling on a plan that would work.

With a few clicks on his keyboard, he purchased two tickets on Southwest Airlines' web site and made a hotel reservation at the Wynn Las Vegas. He knew his troubles were far from over, but an impromptu getaway was definitely going to buy him some time— at least a little.

After stopping by The Den for some liquid courage and thinking about it for a few hours, Tyrese had an epiphany. Outside of having Debbie maimed or killed, the only thing he could do was come clean to Joi. He'd been a fool to think any amount of money was going to shut that bitch up. And even if the investigation came back in his favor, Debbie seemed like the kind who'd show up on his doorstep.

When Joi found out he'd cheated on her she would go ballistic, but eventually she'd get over it. Infidelity was a rite of passage in a marriage. Every man did it. It wasn't like she'd leave him or anything; after all, he was the best thing that ever happened to her. He had it all figured out. While they were in Vegas, he'd give her some extra-good loving and then tell her everything. Well, not everything. He wasn't a fool. He didn't have to come clean about all his indiscretions—just this one.

When he pulled into his driveway, he was surprised to see the house completely dark. It was eight o'clock and Joi knew he didn't like her keeping the kids out this late. He opened the garage, pulled his truck into his designated stall, and killed the engine.

Once he stepped out of the car, he felt lighter, as if a weight had been lifted. But when he opened the door leading into the house from the garage, he immediately noticed the washer and dryer were missing and became annoyed. He'd told Joi over and over again that all major purchases needed to be fully discussed with him before she made any decisions, and especially before she made the actual purchase.

"When she gets home, we are definitely going to have a frank discussion about this," he mumbled.

When Tyrese switched on the lights in the family room, his heart rate accelerated. Where the hell was all the furniture? Instinct took over, and without delay, he moved to the kitchen, then the living room and finally the home office, finding them all empty. Had someone hurt his family? Overcome with fear and confusion, the first thing on his mind was trying to reach Joi. He took out his cell phone and hit Speed Dial. She answered on the second ring.

"Baby, we've been robbed," Tyrese began.

"Robbed? Pu-lease," she repeated angrily. "Being robbed is the least of your worries, especially because my main concern is how I contracted fucking chlamydia. You wouldn't happen to know anything about that, would you?"

"What?" he asked, the buzz from his after-work drinks now gone. His mind was in overdrive, trying to process what she'd said. Did she just say she had chlamydia? That was impossible. Always careful, he'd never had sex outside his marriage without a condom. Debbie was the last person he'd been with, and they'd only had oral sex, but he didn't use a condom for that. Other than that, he never dipped his stick anywhere without a raincoat. That was totally out of the question. He didn't have chlamydia, so how the fuck did she get it? There was only one answer. Maybe he wasn't the only one creeping.

"Maybe you better start with whoever you're fucking because I don't have chlamydia," he said, his voice booming with anger.

"Don't even go there. Besides, I saw you with that whore the other night at that blues club; from the looks of things, she's probably the one who gave it to you. Or shall I say us, you nasty son of a bitch? I also saw the private detective I hired talking to you."

"Joi, wait," Tyrese sputtered, feeling like he'd been gut punched. Joi was furious, and he knew now wasn't the time to try to convince her this was all a big misunderstanding. He needed to calm her down, keep her from making any more rash decisions, like emptying out the entire house.

"Wait for what? For you to try to turn this shit around on me? I don't think so. All I want is a divorce, and as you can already see, I don't want half. I'm taking everything."

Chapter 34

Donathan jerked to an upright position, spilling the contents of the dossier onto the floor. He'd been up off and on all night, and as much as he believed Sydney needed to make the decision to come home on her own, he now had the proof he needed to help her with her decision.

Yesterday, Holsey had given him a brief report on Austyn Greene, which included an address in Oakland. She'd only been in the Bay Area for three months, but the things he'd read didn't explain why she was there and what she wanted with him. Once he settled this thing with Sydney, he would pay Austyn a visit.

Having slept in his jeans, he slipped on a black cashmere sweater, gathered the contents of the file from the floor, grabbed his car keys, and headed for the front door. He had contemplated phoning Sydney but decided against it, feeling the element of surprise would work in his favor. Once he'd learned she wasn't staying at Payton's, he'd called the credit card company and learned she was staying at the Waterfront. He'd had enough of her rebellion and his plan was simple: He'd wait outside the hospital until she emerged and follow her back to her hotel room to retrieve her things and to settle this business about Austyn once and for all.

By the time Donathan pulled his Mercedes into the parking lot of Children's Hospital, he was a few minutes late for the shift change. He wheeled into an empty parking space closest to the physicians' exit, hoping he hadn't missed her. He scanned the parking lot and noticed her Range Rover tucked away in the back row.

A light tap on the passenger's side window startled him.

"Excuse me, sir, but you can't park here. This lot is reserved for physicians only."

He rolled down the window and leaned across the center console to get a better look at the security guard's name tag. "Good morning, Albert," Donathan said, noticing a flicker of recognition cross the man's face. "It's been a while, but I'm—"

"The sex doctor," Albert finished, extending his hand through the window to shake Donathan's hand.

"Yes, I am." Donathan stifled a laugh. This was the second time he had been recognized by hospital security. First at Alta Bates and now here.

"Albert, I wanted to sit here and wait for Dr. James to get off work. But if it's a problem, I can pull onto the street and wait there."

"It's not a problem at all if I can get an autograph." Albert grinned. "But Dr. James left about ten minutes ago."

"Are you sure? I see her truck's still parked in the back row," Donathan said as he reached into the glove box to remove a 5 x 7 glossy.

At that moment the door to the hospital opened and Dr. Julia Stevens, a tall, fortysomething woman with fire-red hair came out. "Albert, have you seen Dr. Day?" she said sharply.

"Yes, ma'am. He left with Dr. James about ten minutes ago. I think I heard them mention something about Lois the Pie Queen."

"Thanks," Julia said, her eyes darting back and forth, as if she were adding up something in her head. "Those two sure seem to be spending an awful lot of time together," she added before she tossed her tote bag over her shoulder and walked away.

Donathan's first inclination had been to just go to the Waterfront Hotel and wait for Sydney there. But he hadn't expected to hear that his wife had left the hospital with a *he*, and what did the redhead mean by, "Those two sure seem to be spending an awful lot of time together." Poised with a Sharpie, he glanced up at Albert, who looked as if he'd intercepted his thoughts.

"Yeah, she was headed over to Lois the Pie Queen."

"Anybody special I should make this out to?" Donathan managed to ask.

"Your friend, Albert." He grinned.

Donathan scribbled on the picture and handed it to him.

"Thanks, Dr. James," he said, admiring the inscription. "And I want to apologize for Dr. Stevens's rudeness. She's a miserable woman who tries to make everyone else miserable right along with her."

"It's cool, man. Don't worry about it." Donathan smiled, feigning to be unaffected by the comments, although he couldn't wait to get out of there. He needed to get to Lois the Pie Queen to see with his own eyes what was going on.

Gripping the steering wheel, Donathan exited the parking lot; his size thirteens jammed on the accelerator. His jaw tightened as he maneuvered the car toward 60th Street. Was this Dr. Day the reason Sydney hadn't returned his calls all week? Blinded by a sudden rush of jealousy, Donathan couldn't think straight. The last thing his wife needed right now was a shoulder to cry on. He knew that game all too well and had played it many times himself. And if the doctor was good, then a week was more than enough time to seal the deal. He looked over at the file folder sprawled across his passenger seat. Austyn Greene would have to wait. His wife was spending time with another man; that definitely was his first priority.

Chapter 35

The rain had stopped, but the temperature had dropped more than twenty degrees, making it feel more like early fall than late spring. Sydney was still wearing scrubs underneath a purple cashmere wrap sweater. She resembled a college coed with a headband holding her slicked-back hair off her makeup-less face.

Lois the Pie Queen was filled to capacity with seniors and couples. Sydney ordered grits, eggs, and chicken apple sausage, and Miles ordered the Reggie Jackson special with pork chops instead of the usual breakfast meats.

She studied Miles candidly as she sipped her cup of tea and listened to him talk on his cell with his daughters. She thought back to how he'd taken care of her over the last week, especially when she'd drowned her marital sorrows in one glass of wine too many and awoken from her alcohol-induced stupor to find his body spooned into hers. It was she who'd initiated the closeness, but it was he who had the sense to stop her.

"C'mon, let me take you back to your hotel room," Miles said, ending his call and pulling Sydney from her thoughts.

"But we haven't eaten yet."

"I know, but we've got company," he said, nodding toward the front door.

For a moment Sydney was paralyzed and speechless. She'd

known Donathan would show up sooner or later, and to say he was furious was putting it mildly. His eyes were dark and irate. He maneuvered around a few tables, pulled up a chair, then sat down.

They engaged in a stare down, her anger resurfacing. She'd never been so humiliated in her entire life and it was all Donathan's fault. Although the furor surrounding his internet stardom had died down a bit, this was the first time she'd talked to him face to face since she'd stormed out of the house almost a week earlier. She felt like slapping the shit out of him.

"What the hell are you doing here?" she asked curtly.

"You didn't give me much of a choice. You haven't taken my calls, and from the looks of this cozy little arrangement, I should be asking you that question," he said, his body language hard and rigid.

Silence descended over the table as the server appeared, balancing another basket of biscuits and two full plates.

Miles noticed the smirks and stares from the other patrons and did his best to diffuse the situation before it got out of hand. "Uh, can you get us the check and pack those up to go?"

Donathan's gaze shifted, sized Miles up, and decided the situation was far worse than he'd suspected. Miles looked like a lovesick puppy—a man who was definitely in serious like with his wife.

"What the fuck is going on here?" he hissed into Sydney's ear. She leaned away.

"I've sat outside for at least fifteen minutes, watching through the window as this man touched you in ways I feel are inappropriate."

"Was the touching you did at Mimosa appropriate?" she spat back, refusing to let him intimidate her.

"Those pictures don't prove a damn thing."

"They're all the proof—"

"You want proof?" he said before he removed the envelope with copies of some of the paperwork he'd received from Holsey from his back pocket and placed it in front of her. "Here's your proof. But we're not talking about me right now. Did you fuck him?"

Sydney stared back at him with a blank expression on her face. She hadn't fucked Miles, but it wasn't because she hadn't wanted to.

"Let's go now." Donathan stood up, and reached for her arm, but she pulled it away.

"Get your hands off me."

Miles rose to his full height. "Listen, man," he began, "there's no need to make a scene."

"If I were you, playa, I'd shut the fuck up and leave because I'm trying real hard not to make this about you."

Miles shook his head, a sheepish grin spread across his face. "Me? I was wondering how long it would take your slick ass to show up, and here you are a week later, raging and fuming and blaming everybody but yourself."

"Who the fuck do you think you are?" Donathan said, closing the space between them. "This is my goddamn wife."

"Maybe you should have been acting like it."

"Motherfucker, you don't know me."

"Unfortunately, I know more about you than you think."

This time when Donathan reached for Sydney's arm, he tightened his grip, not permitting her to escape his grasp.

"Get your damn hands off me," Sydney growled. "You're hurting me."

"Is he why your ass hasn't been home in over a week?"

"Man, take your hands off her."

Donathan swung first. With fists flying, Donathan and Miles slammed each other against tables and collided with chairs, sending patrons scrambling to get out of their way.

"Stop it!" Sydney tried to place her body as a barrier between the two men. A closed fist stung her forehead with a solid whap and knocked her backward into the counter. Everything around her moved in slow motion, but her eyes blinked rapidly, fighting the urge to close in to darkness. Tables were overturned and people scurried to find shelter. After she regained her bearings, she grabbed her purse and the photo envelope from the table, backed out the front door, and took off, running toward Children's Hospital.

Chapter 36

After she reached Brea's voice mail, Sydney hung up, put the truck in drive, and sped out of the parking lot, headed toward the Waterfront Hotel. Her adrenaline was surging and she needed to talk to somebody.

Her hand trembled as her fingers brushed across her forehead, their tips pressing gently on the egg that had formed. But at that moment she was worried less about her head and more about what she'd left behind at the restaurant: two grown men coming to blows because of her.

"What have I done?" she said, isolated by the silence inside the SUV. Without the clutter of outside noise to distract her, she drove down Broadway, thinking about her life and how she'd gotten here over the past week. By the time she reached 2nd Street, the Amtrak railroad crossing gates were down.

Sydney waited, wishing she were going wherever the train was headed. Why had she sat there frozen when Donathan asked her if she was sleeping with Miles? She closed her eyes and inwardly cursed herself. It was so like her to run at the first sign of trouble, which is exactly what she'd done on more than one occasion in the past seven days. Running wasn't going to change anything, and no matter what the outcome, she would have to talk to Donathan.

Initially, she'd been totally unprepared for the degree of attraction she had to Miles and, albeit subtle, if she was being honest with herself, she'd been aware all along that Miles wanted her. It was the cat-and-mouse game that made it exciting and she'd fought it hard, even tried to set him up with Payton. But it all had come crashing down around her last Saturday night.

With her mind still in a fog from the overconsumption of wine, she'd awakened in her hotel room with Miles lying next to her. The sexual tension was thick and her wifely inhibitions were gone. She'd kissed him lightly, and before long he was wide awake and greedily kissing her back. Her memory of the sensations, as she relived the ragged breaths that echoed in her head, was so intense that her stomach muscles tightened.

She had no right to be even mildly upset with Donathan after what she'd done. This was no longer just about the rumors of his infidelity and the pictures on the internet; she'd acquired a suitcase full of baggage all her own. At this point they were both guilty. The pain she'd seen etched on his face—was that it? Was she trying to hurt him like he'd hurt her? Her silence had spoken volumes and she knew the conclusion he'd come to.

Her life was a big mess and Sydney realized she had plenty to think about before she made any rash moves. She needed to talk to someone who'd help her figure out what to do, and if anyone could help her sort things out in a matter-of-fact way, it was Payton.

She arrived at the hotel and waited for the valets to approach the SUV. She released her ponytail and raked her hair across her forehead to hide her battle wound before she was escorted from the vehicle. She made a beeline to her suite.

Once inside, she placed her purse and the envelope she had received from Donathan on the coffee table and pulled out her phone. She punched in Payton's number and began tossing her belongings into the small suitcase that rested on the luggage rack.

"This is a surprise," Payton said, her voice thick with sarcasm.

"How can it be a surprise . . . you knew I'd call you back sooner or later."

"Well, since you've been ignoring me, I'd assumed it would be later."

"I need to talk to somebody I can trust," Sydney said, picking up her personal items from the vanity. "Can I come over for a minute?"

"Oh, so now you trust me?"

"Did I say that?" Sydney mumbled, wondering how much of Payton's ragging she'd have to endure, especially because she knew Payton wouldn't let her off the hook easily.

"Um, yeah, you did."

"Look, Payton, I don't want to talk about this over the phone."

"Well, if I were home, you coming over would be fine, but since I'm in Las Vegas—"

"Vegas? Since when?"

"I caught a late flight last night. You obviously didn't listen to my message, did you?"

"No." Sydney felt guilty; she'd purposely sent Payton's last call into voice-mail oblivion.

"So, what's going on?" Payton asked.

"It's nothing." Sydney sighed heavily, releasing her disappointment. What was she going to do now? She didn't want to ruin Payton's getaway with her troubles. Maybe Brea would call her back soon, and if not, they could just talk about this mess when Payton got back.

"Sydney, I hate it when you do that. You obviously called me about something, so just say it already; I'm not in the mood to guess. And can I have the short-and-sweet version, please?"

"Okay, well, um, in a nutshell, I let Miles lick my kitty and Donathan—"

Payton interrupted sharply. "Excuse me, but did you just say you let Miles lick your kitty? Would that be the same Miles you were so eager to set me up with?" She was now laughing hysterically. "Well?"

"Well, what?"

"Was it good?" Payton snickered.

"Can I finish, please?" Sydney was irritated and eager to get the rest of her story out. She knew this would be the initial reaction she'd get, but when it was all said and done, Payton would give it to her straight, which was just what she needed. "Donathan showed up while we were having breakfast this morning and now I have a big red hickey on my head."

"Did he hit you?"

Sydney thought about the question before she answered. "Well, yeah, he sorta did, but not intentionally."

"Don't you dare make excuses for him! I never would have guessed in a million years that he would put his hands on you. No man should ever put his hands on a woman, no matter what the circumstances. Have you called the police?"

"Slow down, Payton." Sydney was touched by how protective her friend was being. She took another look around to make sure she had her shoes, toiletries, phone, and computer cords before plopping herself down on the couch in the sitting area. "I was trying to break up the fight and I got hit in the process."

"They fought? Oh, damn. I would have paid to see that altercation."

Sydney cleared her throat. Waited.

"Sorry. Go on, tramp. I want the full details."

"Who are you calling a tramp?"

"Oh, come on, Sydney. I don't know why you think you have to be perfect all the time. Not everyone is required to be committed for life. Now spill it."

Sydney sighed. She didn't care how Payton sliced it. She wasn't a tramp, a slut, or any of those other words used to put women down. She'd just got caught up in a bad situation that felt damn good.

"Hello?"

"I was feeling sorry for myself and Miles took me to lunch last Saturday. I had a few glasses of wine too many. I can't remember exactly how it happened. Well, yes, actually I can. He helped me to my room and I didn't want to be alone, so I asked him to stay with me. I guess I dozed off for a while, but when I woke up, he was lying there next to me with his groin pressed into my behind, and I-I just lost it." She took a huge gulp from the half-empty water bottle sitting on the table.

"This is all Donathan's fault. I've never thought about or been in a situation to cheat on his sorry ass, but not only has he cheated on me, that shit is all over the fucking internet and my life is fucked up because of it."

"Um, I hate to be the one to break this to you, but that woman with your husband on the internet is a stalker," Payton said, registering that Sydney still didn't have a clue. She decided not to mention the part about the chick showing up in Pittsburg yesterday . . . she didn't have enough information on that yet to share.

"A stalker?"

"I've been trying to tell you that for over a week, but your stubborn ass ignored my phone calls and wouldn't talk to me."

A stalker? Donathan had been trapped by a stalker?

Sydney reached for the envelope she'd taken from the restaurant and opened it. She dumped the contents into her lap and groaned before she unfolded the pieces of paper and began reading. One minute she'd been devastated with Donathan for his indiscretions and the next she was wallowing in her own self-contempt. What the hell had she done? From the looks of things, all Donathan had done was get caught up in the web of a psycho bitch named Austyn Greene.

"Sydney? Are you there?"

"Yeah, I'm here."

"Did you screw him?"

"No, I didn't. But it wasn't because I didn't want to."

"Then it's settled. It was just oral sex, Sydney. It didn't mean anything and you definitely don't have to say anything to Donathan about it."

"I think he already knows."

"Did you tell him?"

"No, but the way he looked at me earlier—"

"Look, Syd, you just need to keep your mouth shut. This is the type of shit you need to take to your grave."

"Are you okay?"

"Yes. I'll be fine," she lied.

Oral sex might be a free act to Payton, but sharing bodily fluids with someone was something she took seriously, and she hadn't been able to think about anything else since she'd done it. How was she supposed to keep it from Donathan? Nothing good could ever come from keeping this type of secret.

"How long are you going to be in Vegas?"

"A few days. Are you coming?"

Sydney thought about it for a moment. A quick trip to Vegas sounded nice and would give her the opportunity to put some distance between herself and both Donathan and Miles. Her mind was a ball of confusion, but she needed to straighten this out before it got further out of hand.

"Where are you staying?"

"The Palms."

"I love that hotel."

"I know. You should see my view of the Strip. Do you need me to come home?"

"No. I'll be fine. Enjoy your getaway; I'll call you back later."

After hanging up the phone, Sydney sat in the room's deafening silence. She repeatedly inspected the papers she held, becoming fixated on the last page, which listed a North Oakland address for Austyn Greene. Sydney jumped up, grabbed her keys, and headed out the door.

Chapter 37

Donathan sat outside the duplex and double-checked the address with the one Holsey had given to him. He'd played the scenario of what had happened at the restaurant over and over again in his head.

Pain pulsed through his right hand, the cuts on his knuckles still dripping with blood. He gripped the piece of paper with Austyn's address so tight that his fingers on both hands were numb as he tried to control the anger the fight had set loose.

The reality of his confrontation with Miles Day sank in. His body wanted to be sick, but he didn't give in to the urge. With all his extracurricular activities with other women, he had no right to be upset about the possibility of Sydney seeking comfort in the arms of another man. Maybe it served him right and karma was finally catching up with him.

He glanced down at the papers again, wondering if being there was the right thing to do, and considered backing off until he had more information. Holsey had assured him he'd have everything he needed to know about Austyn Greene in a few days, but Donathan couldn't wait. His instincts told him he needed to do this right now; no matter what else Holsey found out about Austyn, Donathan knew only he could save himself.

A few minutes later he looked left and right, searching for any sign of the light blue Saturn, before crossing the street. He hesitated in front of the eggshell-white duplex and stared at the apartment upstairs. According to the paperwork, Austyn lived on the ground floor, but he wondered if her neighbors were home.

Before using the key Holsey had given to him, he rang the doorbell without a plan for what he'd do if someone answered. But when no one did he removed the single key from his pocket and inserted it into the gold lock. The door opened easily and he stepped into a tiny entryway, too small to be called a foyer, and shut the door behind him. It was late morning, but the overcast skies made the apartment dark, which made it difficult to see, but Donathan resisted turning on the lights. Instead, he walked down the short hallway that led from the front room, noting how hot the apartment was. It felt like it was a hundred degrees. He started his search in the bedroom, unsure what he was looking for; still, he continued moving through the space, surveying everything.

He felt like a burglar roaming around Austyn's apartment, although he had no intention of stealing anything. He was trying to understand what she wanted from him, which was the million-dollar question, and as a psychologist he knew the answer would never appear in a private investigator's folder. Holsey had done exactly what he needed him to do—lead him to Austyn. The rest was up to him. Donathan moved toward the kitchen. When he opened the first cabinet he half-expected to find an array of poisons, but by the time he'd finished his tour, he didn't know any more about Austyn than he had before he entered the drab apartment. He found nothing of interest. Nothing to sharpen his gut instinct that something wasn't right about this woman. The alphabetical arrangement of spices in the kitchen said she valued order. There were no pictures or other keepsakes and her furnishings were minimal, which told him she wasn't a sentimental woman. Before he could complete his assessment, a row of specimen jars neatly lining a bookshelf caught his attention.

As Donathan moved closer to further inspect the contents of the jars, a deep misgiving overcame him for a moment and he almost fled the apartment. He took a deep breath to settle his nerves. He was in this apartment to find out the truth, and as it turned out, the truth was staring him right in the face.

The bookshelf was lined with thick textbooks, which a closer look revealed to be medical books, like the ones Sydney referenced from time to time. Was Austyn a doctor?

He tossed that thought around in his mind. The books didn't suggest a psychotic woman, but they did paint the picture of a woman with some medical knowledge who could slip a man a date-rape drug and know exactly what she was doing. But then again, any gold-digging woman could do the same thing without having any medical knowledge.

He picked up one eight-ounce jar and then another to inspect the contents, and frowned at the oval-shaped masses floating around in the clear liquid. Each jar was labeled with dates going back as far as six months.

He noticed a piece of newspaper peeking out from one of the drawers attached to the unit, which was definitely out of place when everything else was neat and orderly. Donathan opened the drawer and found a stack of old newspaper clippings, mostly from Los Angeles, but on top of the stack were clips from the *East Bay Times* with dates that coincided with the most recent dates listed on two of the jars' labels.

Lost in thought, Donathan paged through each of the newspaper items, searching for the common theme.

"Damn," he muttered. He couldn't believe Austyn Greene was responsible for this horror. He was so deep in thought he didn't hear a thing but instinctively swatted at the tiny pinch that felt like a mosquito bite on the back of his neck. Before the numbing sensations invaded his body, he made eye contact with Austyn as his knees buckled, folding his long, lean frame to the floor. He fell into a light slumber atop the sea of newspaper articles that had slipped from his grasp.

When he awoke, he didn't know how long he'd been out, but Austyn was looming above him, her eyes dark and full of desperation, and she was wielding a scalpel. He commanded himself to get up, his fear driving adrenaline through him, but his limbs didn't respond. He couldn't move.

"What the fuck are you doing in my apartment?" she hissed before she sat down on his chest and placed the tip of the shiny blade against the bulging cord in his neck. Donathan's breath caught and he held his lungs full of air, afraid to exhale.

She nicked his skin and seemed fascinated with the tiny red bubble that surfaced and trickled down his neck. He could feel the pressure of her free hand roaming around his waistband and pockets. She fished out the contents, his keys and her key, and placed them at Donathan's side, and then she began undressing him like you would a sleeping child. After removing his arms from the sleeves, she pulled the cashmere sweater up and over his head.

"I'm not here to hurt you," he said as if reading her mind. Why was she taking his clothes off? Was she planning on removing his testicles and placing them in a jar like she'd done to those other men he'd read about in those articles? It was clear she was out of touch with reality. If he could stay awake long enough, he needed to get her talking, slow her down a bit. His life depended on it.

"What did you give me?"

"Shut the fuck up!" she demanded as she removed his shoes and added them to the pile she'd started with his sweater. He smiled at her.

"You think this shit is funny?" she asked as beads of sweat dripped down her face.

"I wouldn't go that far."

"Why are you in my apartment?"

"I wanted to get to know you better."

"You think you can just tell me anything, huh? Like I'm some goddamned idiot." She unbuttoned his jeans. She placed the blade beside him, grabbed his pants at both ankles, and tugged hard, backing away from him. She widened her distance and pulled the jeans with her. "I saw you going through my fucking things. Were you following me?"

"You're playing with my life, Austyn. I had no choice."

"Playing? So you think this is a game?"

"The question is, do you?" he asked, watching her pick up the newspaper sections he'd dropped to the floor. Her hands trembled as she carefully organized them, as if she was putting them back in date order.

"So how long have you been a doctor?"

Her body stiffened and she grew still but recovered before she moved past him into a section of the room behind him. Obviously, he'd hit a nerve. Still sprawled on the floor and unable to move his body, he turned his head to follow her but couldn't see where she went or what she was doing. When she came back into view, carrying a tiny black case, she picked up the scalpel from his side and pointed the tip at the bridge of his nose.

"Stop looking at me."

Donathan closed his eyes, trying to block out Austyn's face and the scalpel. He tried to wrap his mind around the reality of the situation. Here he was paralyzed, lying on the floor in the apartment of a woman who cut men's nuts off and kept them in jars as souvenirs, and not a soul knew where he was. He opened his eyes slowly and shifted back into therapist mode.

"Did those men hurt you, Austyn?"

Tiny folds appeared in her forehead and he watched her fidget beneath his direct gaze. After what seemed like an eternity, she nodded slightly.

"Tell me about those men," he said. The drug she'd given him made him feel like he was floating.

"This is all her fault, you know."

Good. She was talking. "Whose fault?"

"Lois," she said, her eyes flaring with anger at the mention of the name.

"Who is Lois?"

"The bitch who gave birth to me and then sold me to men so she could get high," she spat, as if saying those words out loud would purge the filth from her being.

Donathan had expected this type of confession, but it still shocked him just the same. He'd been a psychologist for years, and no matter how many times he'd heard stories like this one, his first response was always what kind of person would do that. Obviously, the person who did was sick, but sick or not, there was no excuse. "Your mother must be sick."

"Sick? That's no fucking excuse. She's my mother and she was supposed to protect me." She slammed the drawer shut after placing the articles back inside.

"Tell me what those men did to you," Donathan said softly. It was obvious she'd been molested as a child. She'd told him that much when she came to his office. But he was in unchartered territory and knew he needed to keep her talking to buy him some time because leaving here dead or without his testicles was not an ideal outcome as far as he was concerned. Random thoughts flooded his brain. One moment he wanted to yell at the top of his lungs for help, the next he somehow forced himself to remain calm.

"I didn't deserve what she did to me. I was just a little girl." Austyn dropped to her knees and started shaking. "Once they put me in foster care, I thought my nightmare was over. I kept to myself, focused on school, determined to leave behind the hellhole of a life my mother had created for me. I finished college and got accepted into UCLA medical school. Everything was fine until those bastards raped me," she sobbed.

"Who raped you?"

"They all did," she mumbled, a faraway look in her eyes. "I was in my general surgery rotation. All I did was try to help out a friend, another resident assigned to cover a hospice patient. She had a family emergency and I agreed to cover for her. I was sent to an address in South Central. The five of them held me hostage for days and nobody came for me. Nobody came to save me."

At that moment he didn't know what to say to her. He'd heard stories like hers on more than one occasion; for the first time he felt sorry for her.

"Lois told me she loved me and if I did those disgusting things with those men we wouldn't have to live on the streets. Mothers aren't supposed to do that, and instead of fucking me, you should have just listened," she said, slicing her hand with the scalpel, the droplets of her blood splattered onto his bare chest—a sure sign of psychosis. Then, just like that, everything she'd just told him seemed unimportant. His thoughts shifted to the immediate threat standing above him. Fully dressed, she straddled him and sat down, pelvis to pelvis.

"Where is your mother?"

"I don't know," Austyn mumbled, hypnotized by the blood she was now rubbing in a circular motion on Donathan's chest. He was fighting to keep his eyes open.

"I almost found her in Pittsburg yesterday, met somebody who kind of looked like her, but when I do find Lois Greene she's going to wish she'd never been born 'cause I'm going to kill that bitch."

Chapter 38

Like a magnet, Sydney was drawn to the North Oakland address. She needed to talk to Donathan, needed to go home, but her curiosity about Austyn Greene got the better of her.

When she arrived at the Cavour Street address, she was surprised to see Donathan's car parked across the street. What the hell was he doing there?

Donathan had everyone else fooled, claiming this woman was stalking him. Less than two hours after he'd shared this epiphany, here he was at her apartment. And how ironic was it that Austyn Greene lived right around the corner from Children's Hospital. He had the nerve to be cheating on her in plain sight.

She noticed the small park that occupied a corner lot across the street, and it called to her. The park offered no playground or memorial, only a single park bench and winding brick pavers that framed a small S-shaped stream. She stepped out of her truck and paused at the curb to listen to the sound of running water, a sound she'd always been fond of.

She sat down on the bench and reflected on how her life had gotten so out of control. She'd tried reaching Donathan on his cell phone a number of times as she drove there but hadn't gotten an answer. She'd even called home on the off chance he was there. At first she'd thought he was too mad at her to take her calls, but evidently he was just too busy.

After thinking about it, she scolded herself for how she had handled the situation earlier. Donathan definitely deserved an explanation, but she deserved one, too. Her usual MO was to run, but enough was enough. She needed to face this crisis head-on. She slipped her hands into her jacket pockets and headed toward the duplex, determined to turn over a new leaf.

Sydney eased up the four front steps of the duplex and found the front door of the apartment slightly ajar. She almost turned away, but she stood on the porch, transfixed and trembling at what she saw through the crack of the door. A wave of fear held her captive, kept her from taking a normal breath. There was blood, so much blood. She closed her eyes to will the gruesome scene away, but when she opened them the picture remained the same: Donathan covered in blood and sprawled on the floor in an abnormal position, like he was paralyzed.

She left the porch and snuck around the house to a sheer-curtained window. With waves of despair, she attempted to think clearly as she saw Donathan, wearing only his boxers, and the woman Sydney presumed to be Austyn standing over him, holding in her hand a blade more than an inch long and sharp enough to perform surgery.

"Oh God!" Sydney muffled her scream, backed away from the window, and dialed 911.

"Please stay on the line and your call will be answered in the order in which it was received."

You have got to be fucking kidding me, she thought, and hung up the phone. She looked around for any sign of help, but the block was secluded. Not one person had passed by in the fifteen minutes she'd been there. As a doctor she'd heard all the horror stories about people calling 911 from cell phones, and here she was, experiencing it firsthand. The truth was, 911 was designed for landlines, and when you called 911 from a cell phone the calls had to be routed to the right authority by the California Highway Patrol call center, which was not helpful right now.

She looked across the street at the DMV parking lot; there

were a handful of vehicles there, but thanks to the California state budget crisis, Saturday schedules were a thing of the past; she doubted the cars belonged to anyone inside the building who could help her.

"Think, Sydney, think," she said out loud. She needed to get inside the apartment, but she also had to make sure the police could get to where she was, especially because they'd be going off a cell site location versus being given an actual address. Then an idea came to her. She was close enough to the DMV, and with all the terror plots, maybe her location would be helpful. She dialed 911 again, ran back to her truck, and retrieved a tire iron from the trunk to use as a weapon. Moving with confidence, she placed the metal rod in the small of her back. She picked up one of the small pavers that lined the stream and headed toward the back of the property. She tossed the rock, the glass shattered, and Sydney raced back toward the front door and watched through the crack as Austyn backed up off Donathan and retreated toward the back of the apartment.

Still on hold with 911, Sydney placed the cell phone in her pocket and entered the apartment. She rushed toward Donathan and knelt beside him.

"Are you okay? Are you cut?" she whispered, looking for injuries.

"She drugged me and I can't move, but you need to get out of here."

"I can see that, Donathan, but I'm not leaving."

"Well, isn't this touching?" Austyn chuckled, leaning against the doorjamb. "The good doctor has come to save her man."

Sydney felt her heart stop and then start again as she fixated on the sharp blade. With Donathan unable to move, there was nothing she could do except stand her ground.

"Why are you doing this to my husband?" she said, not taking her eyes off the scalpel.

"Your husband?" Austyn grinned. "Well, if he had acted like he was your husband, his ass wouldn't be here. He should have just listened, not tried to stick his dick in me like all the rest of them."

Austyn's words stung, but now was not the time for Sydney to have a meltdown about it. She didn't have to look up to know Austyn was no longer standing in the doorway but moving closer.

"Do you think I'm pretty, Sydney?" Austyn asked with a smirk.

Sydney's gaze searched Austyn's face, as if seeing her for the first time. Austyn *was* pretty, just as she'd noticed in the pictures, but her expression was detached and hollow, lacking a connection to the reality around her.

Austyn interrupted. "My mother used my looks to her advantage. Once I was placed in foster care, I thought I was free. I wouldn't have to do those disgusting things anymore," she said, an unstable laugh escaping her. "But it happened again and again. Those bastards even followed me to medical school, but I made them pay, just like they deserved. My plan was almost complete, but you had to come here."

"I don't understand what you're talking about. What plan?" Sydney asked, horrified by the confusing conversation and wondering what to do next. "I'm sorry about your mother and those men, but Donathan had nothing to do with that. This isn't his fault."

"It is his fault. He was supposed to be different. He's just like all the others I took care of with a tiny incision," she said, wielding the scalpel toward a row of tiny jars lining the shelf.

The realization washed over Sydney's face as Austyn's confession became real.

"You're a doctor," Sydney spat out more forcefully than she intended. "You took an oath to save lives, not destroy them, and killing people isn't going to take away your pain."

"What about my fucking life? Nobody took an oath to save me."

A voice burst from Sydney's cell phone. "Nine-one-one, what's your emergency?"

"Four-eight-three Cavour Street across from the Oakland DMV. Four-eight-three Cavour Street across from the Oakland DMV," Sydney repeated. The sound of the 911 operator's voice held

Austyn immobile for a few moments, but Sydney watched in slow motion as recognition and deep anger crossed her face.

"You bitch," Austyn screamed. She swung the blade and caught Sydney square across her right palm. The shock rang through Sydney's head, but she couldn't surrender. She scrambled backward on the floor, removed the tire iron from the small of her back, and aimed for Austyn's knee.

The iron made impact, but Austyn's dominant position allowed her to grab Sydney around the neck in a choke hold. She squeezed. Donathan tried to sit up, but the pressure of paralysis kept him down.

"Austyn, let her go. This is about me," Donathan pleaded.

As sirens approached, Austyn finally released a motionless Sydney and then scrambled for the scalpel that had slid across the room during the confrontation. She got in Donathan's face and through gritted teeth said, "I'm coming back for you."

Heaving with pain, she hobbled up to her feet and vanished out the back door.

Epilogue

Tony and Tyrese rushed through the emergency room doors at Alta Bates Hospital.

"Donathan and Sydney James," Tony said, summoning the older woman sitting behind the desk. He was out of breath.

"Are you a relative?" the woman asked, barely looking up from her computer.

"Yes, we're his brothers," they said in unison.

The nurse gave them both an I'm-not-stupid look, then said, "You and all the rest of these damn reporters who've been running up in here. I'ma tell you just like I told them, I can't give out medical information."

"Look, lady, we know they're here because Sydney James called us," Tyrese roared, slamming both palms flush against the desk. The frustration he was feeling wasn't just about Donathan. His heightened emotions were also about the state of his job and Joi leaving him. He was still in complete shock that she had taken everything except for a roll of toilet paper. He was embarrassed and hadn't told anyone yet; never in a million years would he have thought Joi had the guts to leave him and take his children. His boys didn't have anything to do with this shit and he wasn't going to take this lying down. Boys needed their father, and he would give Joi a few days to cool off. But there was no way he'd let her ruin the lives of his children. His boys were coming home with or without her.

★ ★ ★

After the catastrophic day Sydney was having, she was glad to hear Tony and Tyrese on the other side of the door, making a fuss. She sent one of the nurses out to get them as the doctor placed the last stitch in her hand. Her wound was deep, but the cut was clean. The doctor gave her a tetanus shot and assured her that in a few weeks her hand would be fine. Donathan, on the other hand, wasn't so free and clear. They wanted to keep him overnight for observation, but he'd refused, insisting that Tyrese drive them home while Tony went back to Cavour Street to oversee the Triple-A towing of their cars.

On the drive from the hospital, Sydney sat in the backseat and checked her texts and voice-mail messages. There were no texts from Miles, and she was worried about him. She had no idea what had happened after she left Lois the Pie Queen, and there was no way she could ask Donathan.

When they arrived home, Sydney left Donathan and Tyrese talking downstairs and made her way to the bedroom to strip off her clothes. She found her favorite jazz station on the Bose system, then made her way to the shower and engaged the overhead water tile. She stood under the ceiling-mounted showerhead and melted into the surge of hot water beating down on her. She was too tired to think, too tired to feel, but she lost herself in José James's "Dream."

Sydney was so wrapped up in the melancholy music that she didn't hear Donathan when he entered the bathroom and was completely surprised when he slid into the shower beside her. Without a word, he washed her hair, and she washed the remnants of dried blood the hospital had missed from his chest and then carefully dried the invisible trauma from their bodies.

Sydney wandered back into the bedroom, with Donathan following closely behind her. He helped her into the bed and then spooned his body around hers. She prayed she would drift off and when she woke up this all would have been just a bad dream. But sleep didn't come easy.

There were so many things Donathan didn't know. And there

were some things she didn't know if he could handle the answers to. Mental health issues weren't her specialty, but she would never feel safe until they caught up with Austyn Greene.

When the Oakland Police arrived at the scene, a search of Austyn's apartment yielded a drug used by anesthesiologists to slow down the body and paralyze patients during surgical procedures, which was what she'd used on Donathan. They also found the jars of human testicles, the newspaper articles, and some paperwork on Lois Greene, who was presumed to be Austyn's mother. Now Austyn was a strong suspect in the deaths of two blue-collar workers who'd bled to death after their testicles had been surgically removed. The detectives had made an extensive search of the neighborhood, but she was nowhere to be found.

The police had questioned Sydney about Lois Greene, and she'd assured them she had no clue who that was, though the name sounded awfully familiar. Even though she didn't know who Austyn's mother was, she sure as hell wouldn't want to be her; Austyn was on a mission of payback and she wouldn't stop until she completed it.

Sydney closed her eyes, haunted by the dreams of a helpless little girl who was unable to defend herself from the evils of sick-ass men and a sick-ass mother. Her thoughts were interrupted when Donathan stirred. She turned to face him and looked into his eyes. His voice was faint, barely above a whisper.

"Did you fuck him?" he asked, never breaking eye contact. His face was conflicted with his love for her and all the other things she could see he was struggling not to feel. Sydney nuzzled in closer, intercepting his thoughts and searching for the strength to do what she needed to do. She couldn't run from his question this time. This was her nightmare—her consequence—and the shit was real.

Want more?
Keep an eye out for
SURVIVING THE CHASE
Coming soon from
Lisa Renee Johnson
And
Dafina Books

Connect with Us

Visit us online at
KensingtonBooks.com
to read more from your favorite authors, see books
by series, view reading group guides, and more.

for sneak peeks, chances to win books and prize packs,
and to share your thoughts with other readers.

f **y**

facebook.com/kensingtonpublishing
twitter.com/kensingtonbooks

Tell us what you think!

To share your thoughts, submit a review,
or sign up for our eNewsletters, please visit:
KensingtonBooks.com/TellUs.